He's one of the smartest, the best ... and the baddest.

Since Dane achieved his lifelong dream of becoming a Navy Seal, his life has been packed with action ... but now he wants more. Especially after seeing several of his friends find something – *someone* – special.

On a mission hunting a chemical weapons terrorist, Dane runs into a captivating woman, and everything about her touches his deepest needs. But the circumstances are suspicious, and he can't determine whose side she's on.

Marielle came to Germany for a short busman's holiday, only to end up running away from the very man she came to see, and into the arms of a man she knows she'll never be able to keep.

As their situation slides from bad to worse to desperate, their lives are on the line. And so are their hearts.

Books in This Series:

DANE

SEALs of Honor, Book 3

Dale Mayer

DANE: SEALS OF HONOR, BOOK 3
Dale Mayer
Valley Publishing

Copyright © 2016

ISBN-13: 978-1-928122-79-1

Praise for Dale Mayer

I love to read Dale Mayer's books... keeps me guessing.... I am getting good though trying to figure out who did it.... I am on my fourth book....

...Review left on Vampire in Deceit, book 4 of Family Blood Ties

Dale Mayer's work is always outstanding and Haunted by Death is no exception.

...Review from Haunted by Death, book 2 of the By Death Series

This is a GREAT series that you don't want to miss out on!

...Review from Broken Protocols Series

This is my favorite author I enjoy all her books and I can't wait for more... her books are easy to get into and I love the storyline

...Review from Dangerous Designs, book 1 of the Design Series

Dale Mayer is a gifted writer who now has me hooked as a new fan. She characters are complex and she shares her knowledge of energy work clearly and simply. Makes for fascinating reading...

...Review from Rare Find, book 6 of Psychic Visions Series

Don't underestimated Dale Mayer. Combination of JD Robb and Heather Graham. Paranormal suspense.........

...Review left on Maddy's Floor, book 3 of the Psychic Visions Series

Wow! I read a lot, and I can honestly say that there a few books that I have read that I will remember for years. This is one of those books. Thank you Dale for giving me the gift of this magnificent story. It was both heartbreaking and hopeful at the same time.

...Review left on Skin, book 1 of Broken and yet...Healing Series

Touched by Death is an outstanding novel by Dale Mayer. Unlike her usual novels that contain paranormal activity, this novel is sheer malevolent actions from ordinary humans.

...Review left on Touched by Death, book 1 of By Death Series

Dale's books are spellbinding in more ways than one. She has a unique way with words. Her characters are fun and funny and loving. I love the way the story flows. Her characters all have personality. She takes you from suspense to love, then fear love and eternal love.

...Review left on Second Chances, book 1 of Second Chances... at Love Series

CHAPTER 1

THE EARLY MORNING sky blew oranges and reds over the small village in Germany. Stunning. Dane Carter waited on the hillside for the sun to come up, for the right moment to make his move. The rest of the SEALs were in position. They'd been following intel that a key man in a terrorist group had set up headquarters here. The company Hyack had far-reaching tentacles, one of which was connected to a major chemical research company in California with branches in Germany and China.

Hawk's cry soared over his head on the left.

Dane pivoted, and slid down the embankment. The house was at the end of town. Secluded. It was a 1600s style stone house with small windows and a huge old stone wall surrounding it. The neighborhood was dotted with similar dividers.

The wall backed up against a hill. His position gave little glimpses of the backyards or the inside of houses. They'd been on the road for two days tracking this guy here. He moved into the backyard of the neighboring house.

The house in question was silent. Dark. The backyard where he stood was heavily treed. Dane slipped behind the foliage as a tall lithe young woman walked out the back patio door with a mug of coffee in her hand. She wandered the garden not twenty feet in front of him. Shit. He faded into the shadows.

She pulled out her phone and made a call. Her voice echoed in the early morning air.

"Good morning, Sarah. Yes, I'm here. Pulled in late last night. I did phone you, but you were out gallivanting around." She laughed at the other person's response. "How's Mom this morning?"

Dane cursed himself for not having moved a couple minutes earlier. He needed to move soon.

The woman carried on her bright, happy conversation. "Remind her I'll be back in a week. I'm just here visiting with my old professor, Dr. Michaels, and going over some of my work while grabbing a bit of a holiday while I'm at it." The conversation continued for a couple of minutes while Dane sweated his position.

Then finally, the blonde, and boy was she blonde, closed the phone and put it away. With a smile on her face, she tilted her head to the morning sun.

And froze.

"Who are you?" she said in a harsh whisper. Her gaze locked on him.

Dane was shocked. She could see him? No. Not likely.

Her gaze narrowed.

Damn it.

She switched to speaking German. Her voice deep, anxious. He spoke a German dialect, but his formal German was horrible. He couldn't tell how hers was but it sounded fluid to his ears. Hawk's cry came again.

Damn it.

He had to go and now. He gave her a bright smile. "Sorry.

Have to go." And he vaulted the huge stone wall at his side.

She gasped but that was the last thing he heard. He landed on the other side to find himself in the middle of the action.

Just where he wanted to be.

CHAPTER 2

MARIELLE STANFIELD STOOD in the garden, her mind telling her she imagined the whole encounter. That she was still jet-lagged from the travelling and time change. Pretty damn wimpy excuse though.

She'd frozen at the sight of him.

Dressed all in black, and huge and hidden like he'd been, was enough to scare anyone, but it was the stillness, the intense assessment of his gaze that had gotten to her. And the surprise. What was he doing there?

Was he hiding? And how the hell had he gone over that tall wall? She was five foot seven, and there was no way she could manage that. She'd climb it but not vault it.

Then she remembered the gun that had appeared instantly in his hand just before he'd vaulted over, followed by…silence. That had been the eeriest part.

The professor's house was one of these beside her. Did he know what was going on?

Back at the open patio door, she sipped her coffee and wait-ed. Wondered. Hopefully that was a police organized raid and had nothing to do with the person she was here to see. Her trip to Germany had been at Professor Michaels' insistence for her getaway. She hadn't wanted to come as her schedule at home was brutal. Yet she hadn't had a break in over two years and her mom's condition was wearing her down. When the professor had offered a place to stay as well, then she'd jumped at it. She hoped she didn't end up working instead of resting. Although a change was often as good as a rest.

She turned to head back inside. With any luck, whatever was going on next door was minor. She'd come here for some downtime – not chaos. Only with that man and weapon – it couldn't be too minor.

Inside she refilled her coffee cup. This house was owned by a friend of Professor Michaels'. She'd been delighted to find it furnished and with a welcoming basket of essential foods – like coffee and fresh bread. She could do worse than just walk the village and relax all week.

She'd been working as a chemist and finishing her Ph.D. program in chemical behaviors for years. The company she worked with, Tenesco, had an agreement with the university and had worked with several other Ph.D. candidates over the years. She'd devoted everything to her work, and her work/life balance had gone to hell.

Then again, having a life was overrated. She'd been there – done that.

With the heartbreak of a broken romance followed by her mother's deteriorating condition, she valued peace over all at this point in her life.

In complete contrast to her work that she'd set out to do as part of her Ph.D. program, but now of interest to the company she worked for, she'd been developing new chemical compounds that did all kinds of damage to a specific focused area then dispersed so fast and in such a way as to not affect anyone a few feet away.

She'd tripped over this new behavior by accident.

But that new direction was why she was here talking to her old professor. He'd left UCLA a year ago to specialize in chemical warfare. And although he'd pushed her to visit for a holiday, she had a feeling he wanted to offer her a job. Why would he think she'd want to work for the Germans? She didn't get it. Michaels was American and so she couldn't imagine him being involved in anything other than something that would help their country. But she'd been fooled before. Now she worked on the premise of trust no one.

So why had she come?

Finally she admitted the answer. Curiosity.

He wanted to know what she was doing and how it related to *his* work. And likely how it might be of interest to his employers. She knew he was teaching here in Germany as well as doing cutting edge research on similar types of chemicals. But he worked in weapons research. And that was something she couldn't handle herself. But she felt compelled to find out what he was doing and for whom. Had he changed so much that he'd create weapons to be used against his country?

She wanted to know but at the same time, she didn't. What would she do if she found out something unnerving? Unless it was to warn her own country that this type of thing was further advanced than anyone thought it was.

Not that anyone would listen.

Still, if the opportunity presented itself, she'd find out what Michaels wanted – and what he was up to – if she could.

As she turned around to head back into the garden, unable to forget what was going on beside her, the phone rang. There he was. She smiled. "Hi, Professor. Where are you?"

"I'm coming over," Professor Michaels said. "You up and awake?"

"I'm both." She glanced out the window for the dozenth time to stare at the house beside her. "When?"

"I'm here already," he said. "I'm outside and walking toward the front door."

The house was huge, so it took a moment to reach the front window and look out. He was indeed coming her way – and he'd been coming from the direction of the house beside her.

The house where the intruder had jumped over the wall into the back yard.

Odd. Then maybe he'd come from the house on the far side. But at least now she could tell him what she'd seen, if he didn't already know. As she watched him sneak a look behind him and quicken his pace, she wondered just what the hell was going on.

She opened the front door for him.

His face lit up. "Marielle," he called out. "How good to see you."

He rushed inside and closed the door. "How are you?"

All the right words were coming out but the tone was off. Too forced. Too fast. Too jovial. And his eyes swelled as if searching the room around her.

"I'm fine," she said, studying him careful. "What's going on?"

His feigned surprise finished setting off her bullshit meter. "Nothing at all." He motioned at the house next door. "There just appeared to be some odd goings on over there."

"I thought that was your house," she said, quietly walking back to the kitchen to retrieve her coffee cup.

"No, not at all. I'm several houses over," he said glibly. Too smooth. And that information didn't jibe with the information she knew already. In fact, it was just different enough, she wondered why he was lying.

"Never mind all that," he said, giving her a big smile. "The real question is how are you? You've been working too hard again, haven't you?"

She laughed. "I always work hard, you know that."

"I do indeed. And you get paid such lousy wages. I do want to talk to you about an exciting opportunity here if you're interested, and I do hope you are," he said earnestly. "I've been watching your career for years now."

"I'm not sure I'm ready for anything different," she said with a small smile, her heart sinking as he confirmed her suspicion. She hadn't needed to make the trip for a job proposition. "You know how much I love my life in California."

"Ah, sorry your engagement didn't work out – do you have a new boyfriend by now?"

She shook her head. "Single and happy that way, thanks."

"So there's nothing to keep you in California then, is there?" he said, an overly bright smile on his face, his arms moving in such an expansive motion she had to laugh.

"Well, my mother for one, and I have a job and my Ph.D. is in progress. So moving is out of the question right now."

He chuckled. "Nothing is ever out of the question." He motioned to her coffee, "I don't suppose you have more of that, do you? It's been a bit of a rough morning."

"Oh, I'm sorry." She walked to the far counter where the very modern coffeemaker sat on the very old looking but restored countertop. "I seem to have forgotten my manners." She poured him a cup and turned to hand it to him.

And dropped it.

She stared at the gun in the professor's hand.

"What are you doing?" she asked in a hoarse whisper.

"Taking care of business. Not my usual style and pretty poor timing," he said. "But you weren't supposed to see this morning's incident next door – yes it's my house, but I escaped and now that I have you here, I get to really see your research. I'm so glad you came, my dear."

She shook her head. "What are you talking about? I didn't bring my research. I came to discuss it with you, but of course I don't have it with me."

"Not a problem, the company I work for is making arrangements to get hold of it as we speak."

What? "I thought you worked for ChemTech?"

"Oh, I did. Technically I worked for two companies at the same time. I stole secrets from ChemTech until I gained the information my current employer needed. Now I work exclusively for the one. A company whose name I won't be sharing until you are with them. Tenesco has been good for you but they aren't your future. Come to my company. You'll work for me. They have big plans."

Blindly she reached behind her for the cloth to clean up the mess on the floor. She crouched down, trying to think, but fear choked her throat. And his words reverberated in her head. Her work was being picked up? How was that possible? It should be locked down on the server, except for the copy she kept for herself.

She shook her head. All she'd wanted was to discuss her work and some down time. Lord, how did this shit happen?

"Do you even live next door?" she asked as she worked to clean up the spill. "It's such a beautiful looking house."

"Of course it is," he snapped. "That house has been in my family for hundreds of years."

Figured.

"Forget the damn floor," he snapped. "I need you to grab your luggage and anything you might have had time to unpack so we can leave the house as if you were never here."

The gun tilted her way slightly. "I'm going to follow you to make sure you can follow instructions. As I said, it's been a rough morning already – please don't do anything stupid."

She slowly straightened, her gaze on the man who looked a little more unraveled than he had a few minutes ago, yet at the same time appeared to be a little more in control with that gun in his hand. It had been wavering but was now locked down on her.

Nice. Not.

What happened to the man she'd known for years? She barely recognized him right now.

She snatched up her coffee and turned to go to the bedroom. In truth she hadn't unpacked her belongings yet. She was an ultra-light traveller and had hoped to shop while here and fill out her wardrobe if necessary – and she'd hoped it was. She loved to shop in other locations as the fashions were so different. Wearing the clothes after she returned always made her smile.

It was short work to collect her things.

He followed her at a safe distance, not giving her an opportunity to get a message out to anyone or to leave any behind. She couldn't stop thinking about the man in the garden. Was he still here? Would he hear if she screamed? She realized her shady professor had to be part of what was going on next door – had they realized he'd escaped? Or did they not know of his existence? Who knew what had sent them to the house in the first place. But if they did know of him, then they'd be hunting him now. Surely a man capable of vaulting that huge wall was capable of tracking this man to her house. But would he do it in time to help her?

As she carried her single bag back downstairs, she contemplated her limited options.

"Let's go," he snapped.

Damn. Her time had run out.

He motioned her to the front door. She nodded and opened it.

Bag over her shoulder, she jerked the door shut on his hand.

DANE HAD SEARCHED the house – to find it empty. The owner had escaped somehow, even though all exits had been covered. They'd been waiting for hours for the right moment to move in. What the hell had happened?

The light had gone out last night showing the occupant had gone to bed on time. And they'd seen him arrive earlier. No one had gone in or out since.

"It's on a timer," Shadow, the quietest member of their team, said, holding up the light in question in his hand. Sometimes his actions were so invisible he was almost ghostly. "Right house but no one home."

"Yet set to look like someone is home," Swede, the giant beside him, said. "It's an old house, any chance there is a secret entrance?"

"In these old farmhouses, quite possibly. Mason and Hawk

are searching the lower levels."

"Shit."

Swede stared around the too clean room in disgust. "I wonder if Michaels ever lived here."

"According to our intel he was seen coming and going on a regular basis for the last year."

"Then where the hell is he?" Swede muttered. "This is bullshit."

Dane understood how he felt. So much time and work went into an operation like this. This was just one leg of a bigger operation. They needed this guy to find those behind it all. Dane walked to the office. He'd done one sweep through there already but figured a second wouldn't hurt.

Someone pounded at the front door.

Dane and Swede melted into the background. The door burst open and the stunning blonde from next door raced in, a small overnight bag and purse over shoulder, crying out, "Help, is someone here?"

She ran past Dane. He grabbed her and dragged her into the office, his hand slapping across her mouth. She dropped her bags. Swede covered the open door.

"Mffmph." Huge scared eyes stared at him.

"Quiet…" he narrowed his gaze at her. "Do you understand?"

Her hands were jammed up against his chest and she could barely move, but he watched her head nod. "Good. Now what the hell are you doing here?"

In a clear concise voice she explained what had happened. Dane was already on the move even as he tried to understand why a beautiful young woman would run to an obviously dangerous man when she was in trouble. It was counter intuitive. When he whispered that question to her, her gaze was clear, her tone concise as she explained, "I figured you were the more dangerous and might save me from him."

He shot her a disbelieving look while he moved toward the front door, Swede following into step beside him. "Like that makes any sense," Dane snapped. "You're then stuck in the clutches of the more dangerous man."

"True," she replied calmly. "But *you* won't hurt me."

Both Dane and Swede studied her face for a long moment. Dane said, "Stay here." And they bolted out the door after her crazy professor.

"Besides," she called after them. "It worked."

CHAPTER 3

S HE SAT DOWN in the chair at the front entrance, an old Victorian red velvet looking thing, and stared at her trembling hands. She wasn't out of danger yet. And until the professor had been caught, she wasn't likely ever to be. How had a simple intellectual holiday turned into this shit? If Michaels had been trying to get her to work for the same company he was, then why the gun? What was he mixed up in? Was it just research they wanted? And if so, who was the company he worked for? Or was it a shadow company pulling these strings from behind? She had no idea what kind of chaos he was involved in. And was her research being stolen right now? How could she stop it from happening? Or as he'd implied, was it already too late? She had copies herself but hated to think that all the years of her hard work had fallen into the wrong hands...

How was it she hadn't seen this side of him before? And if the men hadn't pulled this raid on his house this morning, would she have seen it today? Would he have remained kind and courteous and probed to see how far her research had taken her? Would he have made a move then?

And what was with these military men in the professor's house? They were Americans, she was sure from the look of them and their accents, but she could be wrong, she was a chemical specialist not a linguistics expert. Then again would Americans be involved in a raid here in Germany? Maybe with a joint task force?

She was grateful they were here because by doing what they'd done, they'd forced the professor to show his hand and thus saved her.

She really did owe them her thanks.

At the same time, her gaze landed on an open door beside her. It looked like an office, probably Professor Michaels' office. Should she look? She had no business looking – really, but after the professor's actions... Curious and perturbed, particularly after the morning events, she entered the office and she opened drawers and cabinets, looking for clues as to what had been going on.

Everything was empty.

How was that possible? Unless the house was a front. She frowned considering the size of it. That was a very elaborate front then. She leaned against the wall full of books, her gaze caught on something odd. The wall wasn't symmetrical. The one she was leaning against was too close.

That triggered a memory from a class she'd attended where Professor Michaels laughed about the old house he inherited with secret rooms. It had been used to hide Jews during World War II. Was it this house?

She turned to study the wall.

There were a series of bookends that looked possible. She started pulling, tugging and generally moving anything moveable to find a mechanism to open a hidden door.

The last bookend made a creaking sound and shuffled under her grasp.

"Ah hah." She gasped as the bookshelf opened to show another room. This one, a well-used office.

"Well, isn't this interesting."

She spun around to see two more men dressed in black, the same as the first men, suspicion on their faces. She flushed. "Sorry. I couldn't resist looking for a secret room."

"Really?" the first man snapped. "Who the hell are you, and why would you even consider that there'd be a secret room?"

"Oh," she said, realizing they didn't know anything. She filled them in on her morning, another two men arriving midway through her explanation. The big blond she'd met outside shifted past the other men and moved into the secret room. "What else did he say in that class?" he asked.

"I've been trying to remember but my memory is sketchy. I know he said the house was full of secrets."

At a glance behind her to the others, he made a motion and everyone scattered. "We'll have to see what we can find."

He turned to look at the well-used office space she'd found and added, "This is a great place to start."

"I can help," she said, walking to the desk. "What are you looking for?"

"Anything…" but his voice was odd.

She turned to face him and read the suspicion on his face. "You don't trust me?"

He snorted. "I don't know you."

"True, but then again, you were the one in my garden not the other way around." She smiled and held out her hand. "Marielle, Stanfield. Chemistry Ph.D. student at UCLA and Tenesco."

He shook her hand and said, "And your relationship to the

owner of the house?"

She gave him a brief explanation including when she'd arrived and where she'd come from.

He nodded. "We'll have more questions later. But first, do you know anything about this office?"

She studied the books on the shelves in front of her. Chemistry books. "He worked in here. Not his lab of course, but this was his office." She pointed out the books. "All chemistry books."

And a huge selection. Interesting. She wandered the shelf and back again. Her own professional curiosity peaked. There were some really old tomes on this shelf. As in expensive collector items.

Her fingers itched to open them up and see what gems lay inside. On the other hand, she didn't dare do anything to arouse more suspicion directed her way. Walking back to the desk where the big man was opening drawers at a rapid rate, she asked, "Is there something specific you're looking for?"

"Oh, I don't know. Where he's gone? Who he works with? What he's really doing here?" He snorted. "I'm not looking to find out how he takes his coffee."

There wasn't much to say to that. There was an odd panel on the other wall. She walked over and studied the mechanism in the front of it. And pushed the largest of the buttons. Instantly, a panel opened up and showed a big monitor behind it. She could hear humming as the computer flared to life.

"How about this? Does this interest you?"

He was at her side in an instant. "How did you know this was here?"

"I didn't." She motioned to the tall desk. "I've just started using a standing table myself and wondered at its positioning here. Then pushed that big black button." She pointed to it.

"So it's built into the wall. Why do I think he really meant house of secrets?"

"Yeah," she said dryly. "There's likely to be a lot of other things like this." The monitor flashed up and active. Asking for a log in.

"I don't suppose you know what the password is?" He stared at the screen.

"You know...maybe." She typed ChemistryRocks into the password request box. And didn't the damn screen start scrolling.

"You know his password?" Now the suspicion was truly directed her way.

"Yeah, see in class he had this phrase he repeated over and over again. 'Chemistry Rocks.' He joked that he should use it as a password because he'd never forget it."

"That's not normal to tell people things like that."

"But I doubt he expected any one of his students to actually *be* at his computers. And besides, we don't know that anything important is here." She gestured to the clean desktop screen now showing. "He doesn't keep much on his desktop."

"Move over," he said in a hard voice.

She stepped aside willingly for him to make his own discoveries and take the heat off of her. She had no intention of getting mixed up in any more of this. Her cell phone went off.

She glanced at the number and gasped.

"What is it?" he asked.

"It's him. He's calling me."

The man spun around and stared at her. "Answer it."

Hesitantly she hit answer and said, "Hello?" She held the

phone out so the man could hear the conversation too.

"Hello, Marielle. Sorry we didn't get a chance to chat this morning. I was a little more concerned with getting away."

"I don't understand what's going on?" she cried. "I came here to see you and you pulled a damn gun on me." In truth, righteous anger was getting the better of her. She'd spent a horrible day travelling, looking forward to the visit and a short holiday and look what had happened.

"Well, if those men hadn't come and ruined my morning, then I wouldn't have had to ruin *your* holiday, would I? We could have had a nice visit, and I might have been able to persuade you to come and work for us."

"And do what?" she asked. "You knew I wasn't looking to change jobs."

"No, but we didn't get a chance to talk terms now did we? And my employer is paying great wages."

"I'm not interested in money," she said wearily. "I never was."

"No, I understand that. It doesn't matter now, the game has changed." His voice turned ugly. "You see, you *will* work with me now and you *won't* get paid. But if you're lucky, your mother will get to live."

He hung up.

SHIT, TALK ABOUT a game changer.

Dane stared at the regal looking blonde and knew she was trying to hold the tears back. A threat against family was never easy.

He grabbed the cell phone and realized there was no number

showing on the caller ID. Of course, it would be a throw away phone anyway. As he watched, she slowly collapsed into the closest chair and whispered, "Oh my God, what have I done?"

He couldn't be sure what she was talking about. He'd already contacted the other team members about the call. Now with his phone safely away, he needed her to open up. To see what was going on.

"Have you *done* something?" he asked in as gentle a voice as possible.

She shot him a fulminating look. "No. I haven't. I came here to have a professional visit with a colleague. And see his work. Talk about my studies." She threw out her hands and said, "Apparently he was wanting to convince me to work for his company. Likely adding my research to his. I had a suspicion of something similar but…"

"Yours?" he pounced on her words.

"Yes, my latest study has chemical weapon applications. I didn't intend for that to be the direction of my work, but it appears to be heading there regardless."

She ran a hand over her face. "My mother, I have to warn my mother."

"I need your full name, her name and both your addresses and we'll get on it," he said. "Chances are he's not interested in hurting her as much as using her for leverage."

"If I could get her away safe, I'd just tell to him leave me alone." She pulled out a notebook and wrote down the information then ripped the page off and handed it to him. "Can you stop him from going after my mother?"

"If it isn't her it will be someone else close to you." He shot her a hard look. "This isn't the time to hold back. Honestly, your excuse for being here sounds a little thin."

The broken sound that came out of her mouth made him wince. "I work. That's what I do in my life. I work all day and do research and paperwork all evening – and look after my mom."

He waited, hoping there was more of an explanation coming.

"When he offered me this place for the week as a holiday and a professional opportunity I grabbed it. I was burning out," she admitted. "I needed to get away. So what seemed like a too good to be true opportunity...was."

"And your mother? Is there a reason he'd know about her?"

She nodded. "I'm an only child and my mother is sliding into dementia. She's not full blown yet but is not fully functioning either. She lives in an apartment beside me and has a part-time caregiver. She's perfectly fine some days and then other days..." Marielle stared off into space and never finished the question.

"You're not married?" He was willing to admit he wanted the answer for both his own sake and professional reasons. "Anyone else in your life these guys could pick on? A child? A half-sister/brother?"

She shook her head. "Just Mom and me."

"I'm sorry, that has to be tough."

"Dad died a few years ago and she hasn't been the same since." She lifted her hand then let it fall away. "I don't know what I'm going to do when she's gone."

"You'll bury yourself in work like you do now," he said. "You need to change that."

She sent him a mocking look. "Your world is so different?"

"Well, I do have lots of entertainment on my days off." He grinned. "And my name is Dane, by the way. Pleased to meet you." He winked at her.

Heat flashed in the room.

She blinked.

And blushed bright red. "Of course you do. Being gorgeous and all," she muttered. "I prefer to work, thanks."

"Then you're in need of a serious loving if you think work makes up for sex."

In spite of herself he could see the curiosity moving across her face. She really had no clue. Damn he'd like to change that for her.

But he was on a mission. And she was possibly as guilty as the man they'd chased to his lair in Germany. He didn't want to believe it of her, but...

Just listening to her made his heart ache. She looked so lost. So forlorn. So in need of that damn holiday that had blown up in her face.

He'd love for her to have a real holiday.

But it was not going to happen.

CHAPTER 4

WHAT HAD HAPPENED to her life? "I need to protect my mother."

"Someone is checking on her."

"Can we move her to some place where they can't find her?" In truth her mother wanted to be in a home where her friends were. But on her other days she didn't know where she was so up until now, Marielle hadn't managed to put her into the home. Instead, she'd relished the last few moments they had together.

She needed her mother to be safe. To let her mother have as much clarity as possible. Within months she'd be lost to her own world.

And Marielle was going to be alone.

Forever.

She couldn't quite hold the tears back. She bolted out of her chair and paced the room, crying out, "Why would they do that to her? She's done nothing."

"They won't care. They are building weapons of war."

"I won't build those," she said mulishly. "They are an abomination."

"And what they are doing by threatening you and your mother is also an abomination. If they have weapons you can stop or you have the technology that can create these weapons, then *we* need them. Not the enemy."

She shook her head. "I don't want to create weapons for anyone," she cried. "It's a horrible concept."

"What does your research do?"

"What it was supposed to do and what it does are two very different things." She stopped in front of him and swiped at her overly bright eyes. "I found a way for deadly chemicals to be used in a very targeted way."

He stared at her. "And you didn't plan on doing that?"

"No!" She threw up her hands. "I was working on something else when I realized the chemicals just a foot away were no longer toxic. But at that one targeted spot, they were deadly."

He frowned.

She shrugged. "I didn't think anything of it until other people starting commenting about my work and the military applications. Like chemical bombs that wouldn't kill civilians outside the targeted building for example."

His gaze lit up. "Wow. That would be huge. Chemicals like that drift in the air and are dangerous for hours, days or longer in some cases."

"I know. There is some similar research out there and some chemicals that have similar properties but nothing exactly like mine." She gave him a wry smile. "Still, I hadn't expected to have this happen."

"And you told this guy..." he waved his arm around the house.

"Sure. We'd been exchanging emails for years. I was a student in several of his classes and we stayed in touch. My research took me in a lot of different directions. When he left the university and moved over here a year ago, I never thought anything of it."

"Do you know the company he worked for? The type of research he's doing?"

She snorted. "Apparently he's doing similar work. He wanted me to work under him."

"And give the research to his company?"

She nodded. "And of course he'd get the credit too. Plus, if he's been hired to develop this type of research and hasn't been able to yet, then my work would save his bacon too."

"In other words. He's not going to let you walk away. And worse..." Dane's voice deepened. "The company, if they know who you are...can't let you go. You have research they want."

AND THAT CHANGED the game. She had to be protected. He didn't know if she was friend or foe, but for the next while until they got to the bottom of this, he wasn't going to let her out of his sight. Not if she had the information she seemed to have. No enemy was going to get that amount of research either. Yet Michaels thought he had a way to collect it. In fact, he'd sounded damn sure he could get it.

If she turned out to be a traitor then he'd take her down himself, but until then he'd give her the benefit of the doubt. Only an award winning actress could have put on the performance she had today.

Shadow walked in, and Dane motioned to the computer setup.

Shadow's eyes lit up. "Nice." He rubbed his hands in anticipation.

Marielle made an odd sound in the back of her throat. "I

gather you love computers?"

"Love them. They talk to me all the time and sometimes, like a beautiful woman, I can make them sing." His back was turned toward them so Marielle couldn't see Shadow's face, but Dane watched hers.

The team loved women of all kinds, shapes and sizes. But because of the easy availability, it wasn't exactly a challenge getting them. Now that a couple of the team had found exquisite examples, Dane, like the rest, found himself looking for someone special. He had no idea which member of the team was going to get lucky next, but he wished he wouldn't have to wait too long himself.

Life was lonely. He worked hard and he played hard. But that wasn't the same thing as coming home to a woman who loved him like his buddies did. Somehow not one but two had managed to find special partners like none had seen before.

Now they all wanted a similar partner for themselves. And the standard had been set, with a very high bar.

He studied Marielle. Trust him to trip over a woman who he might not even be able to trust. Mason rescued a brainiac programmer and Hawk found a beautiful search and rescue specialist.

Marielle stared at him, her demeanor changing from comfortable to openly hostile. "What?" she cried. "I didn't do anything."

He raised an eyebrow. "I didn't say anything."

"No," she said, her tone dropping. "But the look on your face changed. As if I wasn't quite who you wanted to be here."

"Ignore him," Shadow said. "He wouldn't know what he wanted even after he tripped over her."

There was a furious pounding on the keys then a sudden, "Come to me, lovely. Come to me."

Dane stood up and walked over, keeping an eye on Marielle to make sure she didn't bolt. "What did you find?"

"An FTP server that he had on automatic log in."

"Hmmm." Not knowing what an FTP server was, Dane kept quiet. They all needed to have a modicum of computer knowledge and he did, but for Shadow, the computers just opened up and talked to him. No one else on the team had that touch. Shadow was known for getting in and out of places without being seen or heard. His nickname suited him.

He knew how and when to move to stay out of sight. The team knew how to move quietly, but Shadow was silent.

Just as Dane turned away he heard an odd noise in the hallway. He was at the door in seconds. And waited out of sight.

The biggest, fattest, orangest tomcat he had seen walked into the room. And stopped at the entrance, a king surveying his property.

"Masters," Marielle jumped up and raced to the cat's side. The orange cat was picked up and waltzed around as she hugged him close. The cat didn't appear to be upset in any way. As Dane watched, the big tomcat rubbed his head against hers.

"Oh, I'm so glad to see you," she cried.

"You know his cat?" He couldn't quite keep the suspicion out of his voice.

She didn't seem to mind this time. "Michaels had him at the university some days. We all loved him, but I used to look after him when the professor was out of town." She scratched the guy's head. The cat closed his eyes in ecstasy. "I really missed him."

"He's big enough to fend off most intruders, but I'm surprised Michaels took him to his office."

"Sometimes he was there for long days, working. We all loved Masters and often asked Michaels to bring him in if he could."

"And the university rules?"

She laughed. "Can't say any of us cared."

He nodded and walked close. Masters grabbed his hand in his paw and head butted his fingers. "Friendly guy."

"As long as you are too. He's a very good judge of character." She squeezed him tight, and the cat's engine kicked in so loud Shadow spun around to see what the ruckus was all about.

"Now that is a big ass cat," he called out in surprise.

Marielle laughed. "Yeah, he is."

The cat jumped out of her arms and strutted over to Dane. He rubbed against his legs and did his best to wind himself in circles.

"He probably needs to be fed," she said, frowning down at him. "Surely Professor Michaels wouldn't leave him behind."

"I don't think he'd planned on leaving."

"What are you going to do?" she asked him wryly. "It's not like you can wait here until he comes back."

"We have ways of finding out when he returns."

She nodded. "And I really don't want to know. Can I go home now? I want to see my mother."

Shadow spun around from the computer. "No, you can't."

She gasped and turned to stare at him. "Why not?" she cried. "I can't stay here anymore."

"You were next door, right?"

She nodded. "I was supposed to be there for the week, but

that's not happening now, so I want to go home."

"Not happening. At least not yet."

"Why?" she asked, a forlorn sound to her voice.

"We need you. You're the only connection we have to the perp," Dane snapped. "You aren't leaving."

And besides, I can't trust that you're not involved yet. But he kept that thought to himself. He didn't see her as a femme fatale. She was too…he didn't know, maybe honest was the word he was searching for. Then again, he had nothing to go by other than instinct. But he'd learned to trust his instincts.

Shadow called him over. "Take a look at this." Dane, after a warning glance in Marielle's direction, walked over to see what Shadow had found.

"It's a series of files. Called Michaels' Miracle."

"That's what he called his project," Marielle said, jumping up to join them. "Those will be part of his research."

Shadow clicked several buttons and files copied over.

"Where are you sending them?"

"For safekeeping so we can take a look at it later."

Shadow nodded his gaze on the monitor, his mind on the implications. "How would a company like his keep this type of research?"

"Under lock and key," she snapped, watching the files copy. "Corporate espionage is a huge industry. Think about warfare and the implications for the Far East."

"I'd rather not."

"Exactly." She wandered the room. "I wonder if he has access to his lab in this house."

"You mean a lab in this house or access digitally to a lab via this house?"

She stopped and stared. "He could have a lab here."

"Could he?" Dane couldn't imagine all the chemicals. "Surely that's too dangerous."

"No more dangerous than any other science," she said. "Still, he'd need the filters and safety equipment." She shook her head. "I don't think I saw anything like that."

Dane wondered, "How hard would it be to hide a lab?"

She frowned. "In theory, not hard at all."

CHAPTER 5

DANE'S QUESTION ABOUT a hidden lab triggered mentions in previous conversations. "He might have a lab here. At least of some kind. But his work had to be done under special filters and with multiple safeguards, it would be too expensive to set up here."

"I doubt money is an issue." Dane glanced around. "It rarely is in cases like this."

"I need to go to my mother." She waved her hand. "My point in coming here no longer stands, so I'm heading to the airport as soon as I can. You don't need me and if you do, you can contact me at home."

She strode over to the doorway and found Masters staring up at her. "Damn, have you been fed?"

Masters meowed.

"Okay, let's check out the kitchen," she said. "I hate to leave you at all, but I'm not going to let you starve too."

With the cat racing ahead, she headed to the kitchen to see if he had food and water. Dane followed. There might be a passage where he could get out and hunt for himself, but she wasn't going to waste time searching for it. In the huge stainless steel chef's style kitchen, she opened the closest cupboards looking for cat food. She found a stack of cans in the third one. She opened one and dumped it into a bowl. There was a bowl of water on the floor so she placed his food down beside it. Masters dug in.

As if he hadn't been fed in a day or two.

Or as if the cans were a treat he rarely got. She shrugged.

She still hadn't eaten. And she was starving. She found fresh bread and butter on the counter. There might be nothing to add to it, but those two elements alone were making her salivate. While the big man watched in silence, she quickly cut up the bread and buttered several thick slabs. After checking the cupboards and the fridge, she squealed at the chunk of fresh cheese. And proceeded to cut thick slices for the bread. She figured the professor owed her that much. The board full, she carried it the table back at the office and sat down. She motioned to Dane. "I made some for you."

She saw his start of surprise and ignored it. She was going to have to deal with the men regardless, so might as well have them on her side.

She picked up a large slab and took her first bite. "It's delicious. Nothing like bread and cheese while in Europe." She laughed. "Not that I would know much about it."

He shook his head. "I'm not hungry."

"Meaning you are hungry but can't eat and shouldn't eat anything prepared by a potential enemy." A sharp pain jolted her. Then she shrugged and added quietly, "I understand." She helped herself to the simple repast until her stomach stopped yelling at her. Moments later she turned to face him. "So what's next?"

He shrugged. "When we're done, we're leaving."

"Good. So I can go to the airport, right?"

He frowned. "We don't know where the professor is. He

might still be after you."

"He might, but he's not likely to do something in a big way in a public place like the airport."

"Why not?"

"It's not his style. Luring me to his neighborhood and trying to kidnap me to stay here – that's his style. Threatening my family. That's his style. Kidnapping me again from a hotel might be his style if he could find me. But blowing up an airplane to kill me off – *not* his style."

"You sound very sure."

"He's weak. Likes money too much, prestige, but he's not a killer."

"And what about the company he works for?"

"From my understanding, they are likely to be the killers. Big money. Big payoffs. No one gets in their way." She scrunched up her face. "Now *they* might blow up an airplane."

"But they need you."

"Do they know that though, or do they just see me as part of the problem that needs to be cleaned up?"

"Good question." He stared at her. "Which are you? Problem or solution?"

"I'm neither. Just someone who stumbled on an unexpected chemical application." Tired and fed up and wanting to go home, she added, "I'm not involved in this chaos and I don't know anything." And as soon as she could shake his leash, she was going to the airport to see when she could catch the next flight out. Then she realized shaking off his leash was likely to make her look guilty as hell.

She turned back to him. "When can I leave?"

"We'll need to talk to you more."

"And you can do that on home soil. Personally at this point I'd like to be back in the US as soon as I can get there."

"Where is home?"

"San Diego." And was she imagining the light of interest in his gaze? Surely not. No, he was interested in her work and how that could help him.

She ran fingers through her hair. She didn't exactly fit into any category, so he most likely didn't know what to do with her.

Returning to the main hall, she found her purse and bag where she left them at the front door. She opened her purse and pulled out her wallet. She searched her purse for the rest of her stuff, relieved to find what she expected inside. She didn't want the headache of having to deal with a missing passport. Putting everything away, she opened her phone and called for the same cab company who'd delivered her from the airport originally. All through it Dane didn't say a word.

He watched her actions intently. She closed her phone and put everything away. "There. I should be on my way home in a few hours."

"I need more information from you." He pulled out some kind of small computer and entered her passport number and her driver's license. By the time he was done, she felt like he knew her better than she knew herself.

"Anything else?" She watched a cab turn onto the street. "Looks like my ride is here."

"No, I have everything I need."

She stood up and motioned to the cab. "So I can leave?"

He nodded. "We'll be in touch."

She smiled up at him. "Of course you will. It's your style."

"What style?" he asked in confusion.

"The whole honorable protector thing you have going on. It's really working for you." She laughed at the look on his face. "Don't worry. I won't share your secret."

"What secret?"

"That you're really a teddy bear." She walked out of the door and greeted the driver. Her protector stood on the front step and watched as the cab pulled away. Just as they were going around the last corner she gave into the urge to look behind her. And found him still staring in her direction.

She waved and watched.

Finally he waved back. Yeah, he'd contact her at home. She couldn't wait.

WHAT THE HELL was that? She'd blown into his life and now right back out. But he wasn't as unaware or as unaffected as he'd tried to pretend. He had no real reason for keeping her. Not if they'd found the files they needed on the computer. Besides, it would be easier to keep an eye on her back home. Hell, he was ready to return himself. So far this mission had hit the pits. By the time he pulled himself back to the present, the cab was just a faint splash of color in the distance. He turned to walk back inside when he heard the explosion.

Spinning around, he watched as the cab was tossed in the air and came down on its roof. With Marielle inside.

His feet were already in motion. He heard other people coming out of the various houses to see what was going on. Jesus. With his heart pounding against his ribs and his nerves locked down, he raced to the cab – or rather what was left of it. Was she still alive?

At first glance he couldn't find her. Then he heard her instead.

She'd been thrown to the far side of the road. Crumpled into a broken looking heap. He ran to her, his hands checking for a pulse. It was there. Thank God. He did a fast check but didn't see any broken bones, but after a shock like that, he didn't want to move her just in case. She needed a doctor. And fast.

Had someone tried to kill her? If so, why? Surely she was worth more alive. Unless they *had* picked up her research – then did they need her any longer? Or were they cleaning up loose ends?

Shadow arrived at his side in seconds. He had her missing bags in his hand, looking crumpled and charred but still intact.

"How bad?"

Marielle moaned. And opened her eyes. Her gaze locked on his face, unsurprised, almost as if she'd known he'd be there. He didn't know how that worked, but he almost understood.

"Hey, don't try to move just yet." He stroked a hand across her face, brushing the hair off her forehead. "How do you feel?" he asked in a low voice. There was chaos behind him as others checked the cab driver over and tried to put out the flames.

"I'm…okay…" she said as if testing the sound of her own voice. "I'm not sure what happened, but I guess I didn't get very far, did I?"

He saw the fear in her eyes, the barely veiled panic in her voice. She struggled to sit up.

"No. You didn't. Sorry." He straightened. "Are you okay to stand?" She should be flat on her back and resting, but she couldn't do that here and neither did they want anyone coming over to check on her. The killer might be watching.

With his help she managed to regain her feet. And clutched at his chest. "So dizzy," she muttered. "My head is pounding."

"To be expected."

He watched as Mason arrived with their SUV. Doors opened and with his help, she crawled into the back seat and lay down. Worried, Dane leaned over the seat and studied her. "Is there a doctor we can call?" he asked Mason.

"Yeah, we might have to wake him up though."

Dane turned, an eyebrow raised.

"He works night shifts at the hospital," Mason said. "Get in. We'll find him now."

Dane shifted to the back seat and held her still as Mason drove through the small village. The doctor wasn't far away, but with the police coming to deal with the explosion, traffic was snarled enough to slow everyone down.

"I'm taking you both to the hotel then will find him," Mason said. "He's likely still asleep."

He pulled up to a small motel. Dane watched as Shadow disappeared into the office. He turned his attention to Marielle. "Hey, you still awake."

"Yeah," she moaned. "But I feel like shit." She struggled to sit upright. "I think I need to sleep."

He studied her pale face. "We're at a hotel. You'll be able to lie down soon." He lifted her out of the SUV. She could walk and talk, but the side of her head was puffy. And he didn't like the look of that swelling.

"All I wanted was to go home," she whispered. "Not get into an accident."

"That was no accident."

CHAPTER 6

"**I**T WASN'T AN accident?" She knew her head was spinning and words weren't making as much sense as they should, but she struggled to understand the meaning behind his statement. She swallowed hard. "Was someone trying to kill me or the cabbie?"

Dane stared down at her. Who was this tall silent man who affected her so. She desperately wanted him to put his arms around her and tell her it was going to be okay. Somehow though, she didn't think anything was going to be okay – ever again.

Her lower lip trembled. She pressed them together. This was no time to break down.

"We don't know yet. Come on, let's get you inside where you can lie down." He reached inside and lifted her in his arms. She cried out at the sudden movement. He paused. "Sorry."

"It's okay. It's just my head."

"Just a little further," he murmured. "We need you out of sight."

She nodded and winced. "I hope you aren't staying with me. If someone is targeting me, you are going to get caught in the crossfire."

He snorted. "Right. Like I'm supposed to leave you alone

and vulnerable to attack?" he asked incredulously, his tone almost insulted. "You did not just say that."

"I don't want you to get hurt."

His next look was dark, directed. "Enough of that talk."

She sniffed and walked to where Shadow waited. "I'm just trying to think of you."

"Stop thinking of everyone else for a change and look after yourself. That was why you came, right, because you need a holiday."

"Sure, see how well that went?" she asked in a pained voice.

Once inside the two connected rooms, he carried her to the bed in the furthest corner. Gently he lowered her to the blanket covered mattress. Laying her head on the pillow, she closed her eyes in relief. She felt like crap.

She could hear the men muttering at the doorway. "If you want me to participate, you need to speak louder."

"And if we don't will you rest instead?" Shadow called over to her.

"Now you're laughing at me," she accused him, her eyes closed.

"No." Dane sat down beside her. "We wouldn't do that. But you can't sleep right now."

"I'm so tired. I can't stay awake," she protested weakly. She opened her eyes to see him staring down at her, worry in his eyes. Immediately she tried to put him at ease. "I'm fine." She reached out and patted his knee.

He covered her hand with his. "Stop trying to make me feel better." But his touch was gentle even if his tone was exasperated.

"Don't want you to get hurt because of me."

"And if you get hurt, who is going to look after you?"

"Doesn't matter," she murmured, her voice drowsy, sluggish. "No one left to care."

"Don't talk like that. You want whatever time you have left with your mother."

"There is no time left. She's almost gone."

THE SADNESS IN her voice almost broke his heart. He also knew how that attitude could impact healing. In a harsh tone he snapped, "I didn't think you were a quitter."

She gasped, jolted awake and cried out, "I'm not a quitter, how could you say that?" But the movement turned her face white, and she collapsed back on the bed.

Shit. "Easy, you need to lie still. Don't move."

But that wounded look in her eyes made him feel like a heel. He stood up and stared at her in remorse.

Mason walked up behind him. Dane hadn't even heard him come in.

"Into ripping the wings off butterflies now?" Mason asked.

Dane sat back down, still staring at Marielle. "Don't you start, I feel bad enough," he muttered, hunching his shoulders. He had a good reason for saying what he said, but it sounded stupid to him now.

"The doctor is here," Mason said behind him. "Move out of the way."

Dane studied the doctor as he walked across the room. He stood up, planning to stand by the door for fresh air, but Marielle grabbed his hand and wouldn't let him go.

He crouched beside her. "It's the doctor. I'm only getting out of the way."

"Is he…safe?"

Her whisper was so low, nervous, he couldn't help but squeeze her hand in reassurance. "He's fine."

But she wouldn't release him, leaving him no option but to stand there on guard. And maybe that was what she did need as the doctor was a big bull of a man. As soon as she caught sight of him, Marielle tried to sink lower in the bed, which considering she wouldn't let go of his hand was almost impossible. He crouched down again. "You have to let him take a look. He's here to help."

Her gaze slashed his way, as if considering his words. She then gave a single nod.

"Hello," she said to the doctor looming over her. "Thank you for coming."

She said it in such formal polite tones, Dane was surprised. Until he realized she was preparing herself behind a front of social niceties for an unpleasantness to come.

The doctor turned to look at the men. "Everyone out. I need to examine her."

Several men went to the door. The doctor's gaze landed on Dane. "You too," he barked.

Marielle gasped and gripped Dane's hand tighter. He could feel the tremors rippling through her arm.

Well, that answered that. Dane widened his stance and held onto her hand, his gaze hard. "No."

The other men spread out around the room. Their stances stalwart.

Mason, in a mild voice, said, "We'll be staying right here. If you need us to turn our backs for privacy, then some of us will. There will always be eyes on you though."

"You called me," the doctor said. He ran a hand through his hair.

"And someone tried to kill her," Dane snapped.

The doctor's eyes widened. His gaze strayed around the room at the men standing guard then nodded once. "Then let's do this fast."

CHAPTER 7

ONLY FAST DIDN'T mean painless as Marielle quickly found out. By the time the doctor had checked her over and poked and prodded his way around her sore body, she was shaking uncontrollably.

From shock or injuries she didn't know. But nausea was sliding up her throat. She closed her eyes and curled up in a ball, trying to force the bile back down. A blanket was tossed over her, the top tucked securely around her head.

"She should be in hospital."

"Is she badly injured?" Dane asked.

"Head wounds are tricky," the doctor announced. "We need to keep an eye on her."

"Someone is trying to kill her," Mason repeated. "They are likely to try again. Do you want her in your hospital?"

"No." The doctor's response was instinctive then he added, "Then she stays here." He frowned.

She could feel the encouragement in the doctor's gaze as if willing her to not be badly hurt so he could leave in good conscience.

Personally, she just wanted him to leave.

"Call me if there's any change. You're going to need to wake her up on regular intervals. Check that she's cognizant. Any change and you have to bring her in."

Marielle tightened her hand on Dane. She never took her eyes off the doctor. *Please let him leave now.*

Mason nodded. "We will."

She shuddered with relief as the doctor stepped back and walked to the door. She was still too tense and locked down, holding on by sheer nerves, waiting until he left the motel room.

As soon as the door shut, several of the men moved outside talking to the doctor, a heavy ripple slid down her body and unlocked her muscles. A long way from relaxed but not quite so frozen.

"Better?" Dane asked, his voice low, concerned.

She nodded, just the barest of movements, but it brought on a boom in her head. Instantly hot tears flooded her eyes to add to her trouble. She turned her face into the pillow to hide them.

"Dane, can you come here, please," Mason called from the doorway.

"No," Dane answered, his voice calm, direct.

She squeezed his hand for a moment longer. Then loosened her grip. "I'm okay. You can go."

He held her hand until she let hers drop down releasing him.

Then he walked over to Mason. She couldn't hear what was said but figured she was the topic of interest. Again.

Still, maybe she could get her emotions back under control. It was over for now. She snuggled deeper into the pillow and closed her eyes.

Snippets of conversation floated by.

"Four hour shifts."

"Shadow is doing reconnaissance."

"Body washed up in river."

She bolted upright. And cried out, her hand going to her head. When she could, she asked in a low voice, "What body?"

Mason glanced at Dane. Dane shook his head and walked closer to her. "Mason has been told that Dr. Michaels, your professor friend, is dead."

"What?" She swung her legs over the side of the bed and went to stand up, but the boom dropped in her head and she collapsed back down.

"Damn it. Stay still."

She stared up at him, but there were two of him now. "Which one of you two was telling me off? That's the one I'm going to give a piece of my mind too."

"What are you talking about?" they both said in unison.

She blinked several times. "Mason?"

"Yes." The voice came from the side, but she didn't turn and look at him directly. "Does Dane have a double?"

"Uhm no," he answered cautiously.

"Uh oh. Then I'm seeing double."

She closed her eyes and blinked. "It's really not fair."

A gentle hand came down to pat her leg. "What's not fair?"

"I shouldn't have to see two of you, you know. It's hurting my eyes."

Chuckles came from the far side of the room.

She opened her eyes and glared at him. "You're really too gorgeous to be two of you. It's not fair." She lifted a hand and added, "Go away."

Exasperation in his voice, he answered, "Hell no. And you're being ridiculous."

"Now you're just being mean." Tears immediately filled her eyes. "I said, go away."

"I'm not going away." In fact, he scooped her up and realigned her down the bed so she could rest more comfortably and sat down beside her. She rolled over and turned her back to him.

He added just low enough for her to hear if she strained and not for the rest of the roomful of men, "Besides, I'm not sure I can anymore."

"Sure you can," she snapped without rolling over to face him. "Get up and walk away."

Determined not to engage in this ridiculous conversation, she slapped a hand over her ear and refused to listen.

She could still hear his snort of amusement though.

DANE COULDN'T STOP smiling at Marielle. Mason stood at his side, a wicked grin on his face. "Looks like another SEAL has fallen," he said in a low voice.

"What?" Dane said absentmindedly, still staring at the woman lying in front of him.

"I said, there's a virus going around."

Dane swiveled and stared up at him. Then caught his meaning. Years of avoiding commitments had him instinctively snapping in horror, "Hell no. Not me. Not now. No way."

Swede chuckled from the door. "Sure looks like it to me. Kinda glad I missed out."

"No, you're not," Mason said in a serious tone. "And he won't either when he gets over the shock."

"Nothing to get over. I'm not in shock because there's nothing to get over." Dane stood up and walked to the exit. "I'm going out. Need some fresh air." And he stormed outside, the gang's laughter following him.

Outside he stood on the small walkway that led to the other rooms. He'd never live this down, and the only way to put a stop to it was to take it in as good natured teasing.

He leaned against the wall and let the night air wash over him. He opened his hand and studied the deep crescent moon indents in his palm.

She'd dug in and held on tight while the doctor had examined her, but she'd never made a sound. And she'd trusted Dane to look after her. He knew she'd be upset if she saw the damage her fingernails had done. But he wasn't. It had shown a level of grit he couldn't help but admire.

He'd seen several women with the same qualities lately, but they hadn't been *his* women. Marielle wasn't either, no matter what Mason said. The other two had been women he'd been interested in, but they'd bonded with his team mates in a big way. Not sure bonded was the right term as it made them sound like owner and pet, and they were anything but.

Still the connection had happened early and fast. And permanent.

He'd watched it happen. Twice. But hadn't ever expected to come close to something like that himself. The trouble was, he wasn't sure that was what he was up against now either.

Besides, he had to stay focused. Someone had tried to kill her.

As he leaned against the wall, he caught sight of a Jeep driving into the parking lot. Hawk. Dane detached from the shadows and walked down to meet him.

"The cab driver didn't make it," Hawk reported.

"Ah hell."

Hawk nodded. "He had a wife of forty years, two kids and

51

four grandkids."

Damn it. It was hard to stay impersonal when these victims became people. It was also the part that kept him doing what he was doing. For the people.

"Anything on the bomb?"

Hawk shrugged. "No idea on the maker. The detonator was on a timer. When it was put on, who knows."

"The driver started his day over six hours ago. So was the bomb intended for her, for him, or random."

"For her." Dane thought about what he knew. "Do we know where he was before this call?"

"Yes." Hawk pulled out his notebook. "He lives only a few blocks away. Apparently he was eating lunch with his wife." Hawk glanced a her. "He's the only cabbie for miles. There was two but one retired."

"So then if she was looking for a ride home, really the best option was a cab and in this case there was only him." Dane nodded. "So that was easy enough but how did they know she was taking a cab and how did they know when to have the bomb detonate?"

"Track her cellphone? Bug the house – both houses?"

"As for how to know when to detonate the bomb? Likely a visual confirmation that she was inside Considering there were two houses involved here already, why not a third? Or maybe the fourth house has guards. Or spies." He shrugged. "Maybe it was to throw us off. Do you trust her?"

Dane nodded. "I do. But it's hard as I don't know why."

"Ah, interesting. Instinct perhaps?"

"Maybe." Suddenly irritated and needing to move on, Dane asked, "What about eye witnesses?"

"The police are canvassing the neighborhood. If they find anything they'll let us know."

The two men shared wry glances. That was the one thing Dane knew wouldn't happen. Chances were good that some information would be passed over but not all of it. Not what they'd need to deal with this.

As they walked up the outside stairs to the second floor, Hawk motioned to the motel room. "How is she?"

"Head injury but nothing broken. She'll be fine."

"Not good on the head injury."

Dane nodded. He used their smart rap code and after the correct response from inside, entered.

Hawk walked over to Marielle. "Hey, how are you feeling? Sorry today ended up being such a crappy day for you."

She looked over at him, her eyes drowsy but alert. "There are crappy days, and then there is today." Her gaze zeroed in on Dane still standing at the doorway. Then she dropped her gaze as if to sleep.

Hawk walked back to Dane. "She's cognizant."

"Good, but we do need to keep a close eye on her."

"We will. We need her. And her research. If nothing else, to make sure it doesn't fall into anyone else's hands."

CHAPTER 8

S O THIS IS what it was like to be watched all the time. She sneezed at one point and the men rushed to her side. All she wanted to do was hold her head against the pain. She collapsed back down, holding up her hand. "It was just a sneeze," she whimpered. "I'm fine."

Except for the damn hammer drill working away at the inside of her skull.

She sat up and slowly made her way to the bathroom. Dane separated from the pack and walked with her. She smiled at him. "It's only ten steps, Dane, I'll be okay."

He never said a word but leaned against the wall outside the small room. While washing her hands she contemplated the shower. She'd love one, but the thought of having a half dozen of the most rugged men waiting for her outside was a little unnerving. She decided against it. With her luck she'd accidentally bang against the wall and have them all run in checking on her.

She could save that opportunity for…say never.

Outside again, she walked slowly to the bed. Had almost reached it when her stomach rumbled. She hadn't eaten much, only the bit of bread and butter and the cheese.

She flushed with embarrassment. "Sorry. Breakfast was a while ago."

"We'll take care of it," Dane said smoothly. "We all have to eat too."

The men immediately started to scrap over food choices. As they were in Germany, she figured they'd likely end up with sausages on a bun from a neighborhood butcher, but when Mason left and returned with an assortment of different foods, she wasn't sure what she was to eat. Had they all ordered something different or was he just bringing in food to share? She watched and waited.

Then laughed.

Dane was grabbing two plates full of food. One for her and one for himself.

When he walked toward her, she shifted to lean back against the headboard. "Thank you."

He nodded, sat down beside her and tucked into his own food. She ate slowly, savoring the food, then realized the men didn't know what that meant. They were inhaling the meal without appearing to appreciate what they ate. She got the impression food was energy and that was how they ate. As if it didn't make any bit of difference what the food was.

She settled down to enjoy her mix of potatoes, veggies and of course sausages. Still the fresh bread on the side was welcome. Now a coffee would top this off perfectly.

By the time she was halfway through her plateful, her head and stomach were arguing. And she was afraid her head was winning as the food started to churn. She slowly laid her plate down and sat up, her hand to her belly.

Dane stopped eating. "It's not staying down?"

She slowly stood up. "I'm not so…" And then she knew. And bolted for the toilet where she lost everything she'd eaten. As hungry as she had been, she was now wishing food never existed. Even the smell was getting to her. She was hesitant to walk back out. Not with that much food around. And as much as she wanted a coffee, that was starting to sound like a bad idea too.

How long was this going to last? Honestly, she felt like shit.

Shaky, she made her way back to bed, all eyes watching her trip. When she curled up facing the wall, she could hear them all move. She closed her eyes and willed them away.

Until there was a harsh knock on the door.

Everyone froze.

She curled up into a tighter ball wishing she could disappear. Go home and forget about Professor Michaels and this trip. Go back to her mother and her research. She hoped Masters would be okay. Then she realized the professor was dead. So who was going to look after Masters?

She heard voices so assumed someone had answered the door. But she didn't know who it was or why they were here. The men would handle it. She just had to handle herself.

DANE STOOD IN the way of anyone from the door being able to see the occupant in the bed. Hawk stood at his side. Both faces, stone hard, stared at the hotel manager. He was upset about the number of people in the room. Dane snorted. Really? In college they'd have had lots more people in a single room. They'd bought two rooms as there was always going to be several men on guard duty outside. There were now. He could just imagine if the manager knew about them.

Mason patted the manager on the shoulder and walked him outside far enough that the others could shut the door and keep

Marielle in the shadows.

Dane slipped to the window and peered out. Mason was still talking to the manager and appeared to be handing over more money. Figured. The cash under the table bribe seemed to work in every country. He glanced back at Marielle, not happy at her color. How could they move her if she was seriously hurt? She'd been fine then all of a sudden she wasn't fine.

Swede walked over. "I just spoke with the doctor. He's not happy with the change in her condition. He wants her brought in for tests."

The three men looked at each other then at Marielle who appeared to be finally asleep. "He can't come here for a second checkup?"

Swede shook his head. "Says that won't do anything. At the hospital they can run some tests. If there is swelling on the brain then that will need to be carefully monitored."

"And the food might not have agreed with her."

Mason walked back in. "Trouble averted for the moment." He stopped and stared at the men, his gaze narrowing. "What's up?"

"I called the doctor. He wants to run some tests on Marielle in light of her new symptoms."

Mason slowly shook his head. "Not a good idea."

"And if she's got a serious head injury?" Dane asked. "Then what?"

"We're supposed to be leaving the country tonight. Going home."

There was a startled silence as the men studied Mason. "Why?" Shadow asked. "And why now?"

"The dead prof. The attack on Marielle. All point to the

company Hyack as we thought. Although based in Germany, they have a factory in China." He offered a wry smile. "Looks like we're heading there next."

They relaxed. "Good. Makes more sense than running around in the dark here."

"And Marielle, what do we do with her?"

"Do we have her passport?" At Dane's nod, Mason said, "We'll take her to San Diego and let the doctors check her over there."

"Then we need to move fast," Dane said. "If she goes to the hospital here it will be hours if not days before she'll be released. We can hardly spring her free if we're the ones who took her in the first place. And if we take too long, she could end up in serious trouble."

"I'll see if I can move that time forward. Departure was originally set for nine pm."

Dane looked at his watch. "Try to reschedule for...how about right now."

"I'll see what I can do," Swede said from the doorway.

Mason headed back outside. "Do you think it's safe to take her with us? To move her."

"It think it's safer than leaving her here unprotected."

"Good point."

CHAPTER 9

MARIELLE WAS BUNDLED up in a blanket and packed out to the SUV like a little child. She woke at the beginning of the process. Her protests about being able to walk fell on deaf ears. Inside the car she watched the others split up into three vehicles and head out convoy style. She didn't know if she was still considered a suspect or if they were being nice and protecting her or if now she was considered important for their case. She knew something had shifted.

It was hard to be unhappy about it. It appeared she was going to be leaving the country and going home. That suited her.

Then she remembered Masters.

She told Mason that with Professor Michaels gone someone had to help the cat. He just stared at her. "Not our problem."

She glared at him. "We can't leave him."

"We can't take him." Final and clear.

"Not good enough. Someone has to know the owner of the house left a cat locked up inside."

"We're on a mission. We're SEALs and that cat is not the mission."

"You're men sometimes, not always SEALs," she snapped, feeling a punch in her gut at hearing they were part of that elite, elusive group. Her comment earned her a hard look. "And protecting those that can't help themselves *should* be part of that mission, Masters included."

Mason drove while she fretted. Dane had gone into a different vehicle. She hated that. Finally they pulled into a military base and papers were brought out. Including hers. She sat in the backseat wondering if she'd be allowed to fly. Did anyone know she was even at the house of the dead man? Did they care if she was?

The vehicle pulled forward and headed for a large hanger on the side. Inside was a military looking plane. As in this thing meant serious business. Organized chaos was going on inside. Nothing panicked but serious directed activity. She was good with that.

The vehicle pulled over and her door opened. Mason scooped her out and put her on a small luggage cart. He walked beside but she was driven to the plane. She felt ridiculous.

"Could've walked you know," she muttered. "Feel silly."

"You look like hell."

That shut her up.

She was carried to a seat up front and tucked in out of the way. After that she sat and watched. With any luck she'd be stateside in a few hours. Like hell she was leaving home again anytime soon. Her head still boomed, but fatigue was the real problem right now. She just wanted to sleep.

Before long the plane was taxiing down the runway. It stopped for something. She didn't know what the commotion was but shortly afterward, it geared up those powerful engines. And they were in the air minutes later.

Now that she'd managed to get this far, she curled up in her chair and slept.

Hours later she woke groggy and sore and feeling like a bus had dragged her around the block. She raised a hand to her head. The booming was still going on but in a background noise type of way. Another noise finally penetrated the fog. She shifted so she could look around and found a cat carrier beside her. "Masters!" she cried out softly.

The huge tabby, well-travelled and comfortable in his personal cage, meowed back. She slid several fingers through the holes in the wall and stroked the animal's silky fur. His diesel engine kicked out the walls of the cage in a distinct hum. She'd loved that cat. She didn't know if she had legal rights to him or not but was happy to foster him until they could find out.

With a gentle smile on her face she looked over at Mason who sat across from her buried in thoughts. "Thanks, Mason."

He rolled his head her way, saw her and the cat and shook his head. "Not me. Thank Dane. And he'll catch hell for it too."

"Oh no." That was the last thing she wanted, but it was hard to be upset with the cat's huge eyes staring so trustingly at her. "Masters and I are old friends. I used to cat sit him at my house when Michaels was still my prof."

"Hmm." But there was humor in Mason's voice. "Never knew Dane to be a cat person."

Shadow, walking over to sit down beside Mason, said, "He's not. He's a Marielle person."

The two men snickered.

She blinked, not getting the jibe for a moment, then felt her cheeks flush bright red. She gazed at the cat, a tiny smile on her lips. Really? "He's very sweet," she murmured.

The men laughed. "Yeah, that's Dane all right. He's sweet." Shadow raised his voice loud enough for the rest of the occupants in the plane to hear. "We should call him that from now on."

Dane came out of nowhere and shoved his face into Shadow's rollicking laughing one.

Marielle gasped. "What are you doing?" she scolded. "Shadow has been a big help."

Dane backed off, rolled his eyes and Shadow lost it, slumping down in the chair, snickering. Marielle turned her gaze to Mason who was desperately trying to hold his own amusement in.

"Dane's really a very nice man," she said earnestly. "He's been good to me."

Mason, his face contorting with effort, managed to keep his mouth shut as he got up and walked to the back. She frowned at his retreating back. Were his shoulders shaking?

Spinning around she caught Dane's brooding glare. She threw up her hands. "What did I say?"

"You called me sweet," he growled.

Her face softened, her hand instinctively going back to touch Masters. "And you are," she said gently. "I really appreciate that you brought Masters."

"I couldn't leave him behind," he growled, "and none of the neighbors wanted him or could tell me if there was anyone left to look after him."

"Exactly." She beamed at him. "See…caring, kind…sweet."

HE SHOULD BE insulted. There was really only so much a man could take. The guys were never going to let him live this down.

Yet he wasn't insulted – not really. Or rather, if she'd said that while the two of them were alone, he'd not have minded at all. Still the guys would razz him good for a while. Then, he'd done his fair share of bugging them, so maybe it was his turn. He closed his eyes and crossed his arms over his chest.

He napped in a half doze, always alert but knowing the trip was going to be long enough and if he could catch some rest, it was the best option.

At the sound of whispers in the back, he sat quietly for the moment then straightened and looked around. Marielle lay draped across the cat cage and appeared to be asleep, but something was going on with his team. He got up and made his way to the back. "What's up?"

"Orders to change course," Mason said. "We've got intel on Michaels' boss. He was just tagged entering Italy."

Damn. He glanced back at Marielle. "Did you explain we have an injured civilian on board?"

Mason winced. "Yeah, she's to go to a medical center and we're to leave her there. The US Embassy will be contacted on her behalf."

The other men sucked in their breaths. That was not something any of them would choose to do.

"Not happening." Dane sat down, his arms across his massive chest. "She needs care and not to be dumped in yet another foreign country."

Mason sighed. "I can only tell you what they are saying."

Dane understood. It wasn't the first time they'd helped out a civilian in trouble and had to leave. Marielle wasn't going to appreciate not getting home. The cat was also going to cause trouble. Shit. "She's too valuable. We can't leave her alone."

"No, but she could return stateside with another plane."

"True. Except they sent her with us."

"Exactly." Mason was back on his communicator. "I'm working the angles."

Dane stared out the window, his mind spinning the options. He could stash her somewhere while they chased after the boss. By the time they landed, intel would be confirmed and a plan in place. They could be in and out of Italy within a few hours.

Or days. Even weeks if things fell apart. She could not stay that long. Even healthy she couldn't stay that long. She'd have to get a commercial flight and go home. With the cat. So more paperwork and more money to get the paperwork through fast enough to get the cat through the borders. His mind worked as the men waited on Mason.

"We're landing in a small airport a couple hours outside of Rome."

So much for a hotel. He'd seen some of those small airports. They were talking dirt strips if they were lucky. And that meant no airport hotel for Marielle. "What if she didn't get off the plane?"

At Mason's sharp look he realized he'd asked his question out loud. He shrugged. "If she stays on board, then she'll be able to go back with us."

"We could be days."

"We could be hours," he countered.

"It could be dangerous."

"She's a target." The best place for her was with them.

"We don't know she's the target."

"The prof is dead. She's alive and she's the one with the research. They want her."

The others exchanged glances. They had a protocol in place for a lot of situations, but they also knew that every mission required adaption to make it through. They'd pushed the line many times. Sometimes to survive. Sometimes because it was the best thing to do. Sometimes it was the right thing to do.

He hoped this time fit in one of those. There was no way he felt good about dumping Marielle, injured, in a small town miles from an international airport all alone.

Hell no. Not going to happen.

CHAPTER 10

T HE PLANE LANDED as she was waking up and rubbing the sleep from her eyes. She stared out the window in confusion. Uhm, she didn't know what time it was, but it surely could not have been time for a transatlantic flight like she'd expected. And neither did this small, flat, rundown airstrip look like an international airport.

Where the hell was she?

With Masters' cage gripped tight in her hand, she turned to look at the men.

Only they were all geared up. Fear shot through her. What had happened? Why hadn't they said something to her? Masters meowed in his cage. She dragged the cage onto her lap and curled up in the corner, trying to still the panic in her stomach.

The only good thing was she was feeling relatively normal. The headache was still there but less a pounding than a dull ache. But...she stared outside in the evening light and wondered what the hell she was supposed to do here.

And where was Dane. He should have explained what was going on long before now.

"How are you feeling?" Dane stood in front of her. His gaze deep, assessing.

"Fine," she said, her voice trembling despite her best attempts to keep it firm. "Where are we and why?"

"We're in Italy. Our flight was diverted as we were given new information."

She nodded as if she understood, but in truth, no one could understand anything given the little information he'd given her. "And me? Where am I going?"

"That's possibly a choice. In theory you're supposed to go to a medical clinic on your own where the US Embassy will contact you."

"What?" She blinked, trying to understand how it was she went from being a protected casualty to a don't-need-dumped-at-the-next-stop, person.

"I see," she managed in a calm, slightly strangled voice. "Then I guess I'd better grab my things."

"Or…"

She stopped in her attempt to put Masters down on the seat beside her so she could stand up. And twisted to look at him. "Or?"

"Or you stay here with the pilot."

"That's a hell of a choice." She eyed him. "Is it safe?"

He nodded.

"Is it a good idea?"

He nodded. "If you want to. Unless you have friends who want to deal with the embassy or a family support system in Italy, about two hundred and forty miles from Rome, then stay."

Not likely. She studied his carefully blank face and knew what her next question had to be. "Am I allowed to stay on board?"

He shook his head. "Not likely. We're not asking for permission. You're here. They know that. We've been diverted for an excellent reason. Makes sense that they'd know you're still here."

"But?" There was more to this.

"It's your choice." He turned and joined his team at the back of the plane, leaving her stunned and confused.

Did he want her to stay? He implied as much. No, he implied she should stay. Not that he *wanted* her to stay. Determined to get to the bottom of this, she stood up and walked to where the men were, only they were exiting faster than she could reach them. By the time they were there, Dane was getting ready to close the door, locking her in.

"Wait," she called out. "I thought you said I could leave."

He gave her a crooked grin that did crazy things to her heart and said, "I lied."

And he shut and locked the door behind him, locking her inside.

With a smile on her face.

DANE HOPPED ONTO the back of the truck. The others were ready, the engine revving, raring to go.

"How'd she take it?" Mason asked from the front passenger seat.

"Not sure. I didn't hang around to see."

But he had caught the relief on her face. He'd made the right decision. She'd been through too much already. She needed time out. A few hours in a plane with the pilot would do that.

The others grinned.

"Now let's get this job done." They had an address in an old warehouse just out of town. Deserted and derelict but supposedly with an operation functioning underground. A good place for a chemistry lab. No regulations to worry about. And being out of town, they could keep their activities secret. It wasn't a production site but a research lab. That meant less staff to keep track of. And quite likely there were living quarters there as well.

The drive was just over half an hour. They were supposed to meet the informant first.

Pulling up to the gas station, they split up and disappeared around the block. Mason, less militarily dressed than the others, walked into the small cafe and took a table at the window. Dane walked in, just in his navy pants and dark t-shirt and took a table at the end of the room. He ordered coffee and waited. An older man walked in. He looked to have an odd illness. His footsteps shuffled and his hands, as he lifted them in greeting, seemed to shake.

Was it from being around chemicals or just life taking its toll on the body that had lost the strength to fight back? He shuffled to Mason's table and sat down, greeting him as an old friend. Knowing Mason had spent years in Europe, he might be.

The two men talked casually while drinks and food were delivered. To anyone watching they appeared to be good friends visiting.

After they finished both, the old man got up and left as if he'd just had a casual visit. Nothing untoward. Yet Dane knew better.

He finished his coffee and walked over to pay for it at the till.

From where he stood, he could see the old man shuffle down the sidewalk. He walked out the restaurant just in time to see a vehicle rip around the corner. He instinctually melted against the wall.

A funny pop echoed through the air. Gunshot.

The old man staggered before collapsing to the ground, a bullet in his head.

Mason raced out of the cafe, took one look, swore and said, "We need to get the hell out of here."

They bolted back to the vehicle. Shadow raced to the back of the vehicle and jumped in. "I managed to catch the license plate." He mumbled the same number sequence several times over as he punched it into a database. The GPS brought the address up in seconds. Dane had a lot of appreciation for his predecessors who functioned just as effectively – without technology. Of course they were up against an enemy that had no technology at the time as well.

"We didn't get anything worthwhile. He said there'd been nothing unusual at the place in the last few weeks. He was willing to get us to the lab but said we'd need to get the local law involved and do an official investigation. He did say that Hyack had sold this lab recently. The sale going through just last week."

"Too fast for us to have known the ink was even dry. Possibly the company's streamlining its operation."

"Or they had nothing to do with it."

"Then why shoot the old man?"

"More loose threads?"

With more questions than answers swirling around, and with Mason driving and Dane running navigation, they arrived at the address in less than two minutes. He drove past the house then at the next corner half the men ejected while he turned around and came back. There were houses on both sides. A small compact car was parked in the front.

Similar enough in size to be their drive-by shooter. The lack of a license plate just added to the suspicion. It had to have been removed after the shooting.

Mason drove past the house again and parked down the road. Dane went behind the neighbors and came up from the side. There were no sounds inside. No lights on. But the vehicle was there.

Dane slid around the house to the back door and peered in through the window.

A man lay on the floor face up, a small circle in his forehead. Dane quickly informed the others then reached for the back door and found it already open. He nudged it wider and crouched down in the dark. Not a sound from inside.

Had he done his job and come home to a reward he hadn't expected? Still, it was very much the same style they'd encountered since this job began. The company was cleaning up after themselves.

Mason arrived beside him and quickly they dove in, guns ready. A search of the premise confirmed Dane's initial thoughts. The house was empty. The shooter long gone.

There was nothing tying them together except Marielle.

Dane stooped down by the body and a strangled gasp erupted from his lips.

He held up his hand to reveal a small heart locket with the word Marielle written across the back. He opened it. Inside was a picture of a young mother holding an infant on one side and a mother and daughter standing together on the other. The young woman was scarily familiar.

He held it out for Mason to see. "What's the chance this is Marielle's?"

Mason walked closer and held out his hand. "Shit."

"I guess it's a good thing she stayed with us." Dane motioned to the room around them. "Although I'm not sure this guy had the locket as much as the killer left it behind as a message."

Dane had his communicator out and called the pilot. If anything had happened to Mari…

Mason waited then asked, "What did you find?"

Only Dane was redialing. "I found nothing," he snapped and swore as he misdialed. "I'm calling again."

"Call from the vehicle. There's nothing here. If the guy lived here longer than two days, I'd be surprised."

Dane shut down the call and raced out the back door and through the neighbor's yards. He met the others at the vehicle, everyone getting in fast, Dane taking off before the doors were shut.

Mason updated the others.

"Are we thinking someone saw us and went to the airstrip to look for Marielle? How would they know we're here?"

"Easy. They saw us." Shadow shrugged at the looks he got. "Small airstrip, military plane overhead. Already taken out a loose thread. Maybe it was just luck on their side."

"Maybe someone tipped them off when we drove through town. These guys have eyes and ears in many places."

"And maybe they are tracking our cellphones or our transmissions. Who the hell knows?"

"We might need to consider that Marielle is being tracked too."

"Not likely." But Dane knew stranger things had happened. Although he knew it was wrong, he had to keep an open mind in regards to Marielle's involvement. "Then again, her cab was targeted. Maybe she is being tracked."

The trip to the plane was completed in record time. He pulled up to the side of the strip and got out. The plane was in darkness and silence. It should have been anyway.

But, the shattered window gave it a completely new look.

CHAPTER 11

THE PILOT WALKED toward her. She'd been patient up until now but worried the longer the men stayed away. It was reassuring to not be alone though.

She smiled up at him. "I guess there's no way to know when they'll come back."

"They'll let us know when they are a few minutes out." He patted her shoulder. "Sleep if you can. They could be minutes or they might be hours."

"Right." She leaned her head back but was all slept out. To pass the time, she walked her way mentally through the chemicals she so loved. She'd had a huge chart of them she'd used as a coloring book when growing up. Obviously she'd known early what she wanted to do.

Too bad she wasn't at home doing it. She stared down at her phone. Could she call her mother? See how she was doing? Would that put them in danger or did no one give a damn? She leaned toward the latter as really, she was no one. She studied the direction the pilot went, wondering if she should ask him. But she didn't want to disturb him. Besides, she might not get reception anyway.

She opened her phone and found three texts. One from her mother's caregiver asking a question about meals. She quickly answered that one, relieved when the message was sent. She had some reception at least.

The second text was a friend at work asking about her holiday. There wasn't much to answer, so she figured she'd leave that one for later.

The third text was from the Michaels.

She froze. Considering he was dead, he couldn't be sending her messages. She'd love to believe in ghosts but until she actually had proof of such things, it wasn't going to happen. Someone who had access to his email account had to be sending this. And that couldn't be good. She clicked on it.

And found an image of a dead man. A second image was of her locket.

She reached up for the necklace she always wore, particularly since her mother's diagnosis. It had been a gift when Marielle was twelve. Now she treasured it.

And apparently had lost it without even knowing. How did that work? Someone had to have taken it off her when she was unconscious, either at the accident or afterwards. No, she wouldn't believe a SEAL would do such things. Not possible.

So when had she seen it last?

And why send her an image like that? She wanted her necklace back but was she going to end up dead like the man in the picture? She scrolled the text and the simple message underneath.

"We're coming for you."

She swallowed hard.

An odd ping rang out, followed by the sound of shattered glass.

From the cockpit.

Oh shit. She closed her eyes. Please let that not have been a gunshot. And not the plane's windshield blown out. *Please.* She slowly got up and snuck over to the window and looked out.

Nothing but blackness for as far as she could see.

Damn. She returned to her chair, was almost sitting down, when the door burst open and two men raced inside. They grabbed her before she could take a couple steps. She screamed and fought back. Her cell phone dropped to the ground. One of the men laughed and snagged it up and pocketed it. "Good, we need that too."

A hood was thrown over her head, and she was lifted and carried toward the exit.

She kicked and screamed. But they were stronger, bigger and there were two of them.

Hanging over the shoulder of one man, she felt the descent as they went down the stairs from the plane. Reacting blindly, she threw herself to the side, causing him to stumble. He lost his grip and she hit the ground hard, knocking the breath out of her.

"God damn it," a male voice roared.

"Can you handle her?" came the mocking second voice. "Or do you need help with such a small woman?"

"I don't need any help," her captor snarled. "She's just a fucking pain in the ass. I'm going to knock her out in a second." He picked her up and tried to shift her weight into a different position. That's when she threw herself back, slamming into his head.

She couldn't hold back her groan of pain as she fell to the ground, and for the second time knocked the breath out of herself. The second man laughed his fool head off.

"This isn't fucking funny."

"Sure it is. She's nothing but a slip of a thing, and she's got the best of you. Twice."

Marielle was still trying to get her breath back when she

heard a single gunshot fire. Followed by a loud thud. *Oh shit.*

"Did you hear that?" snarled the man who had been carrying her. "The next bullet is yours. No one fucking laughs at me."

This time he didn't bother trying to pick her up. He grabbed her by the foot across the runway.

She bounced along still half tied, trying to figure out how to get away. Her best chance would be when he loaded her in the vehicle, but after that she was in deep trouble.

And if she pulled away and ran now, she'd get a bullet in the back. She didn't know who her captor worked for, but she doubted he gave a shit whether he delivered her alive or dead. He'd rather shoot her for escaping than face his bosses as a failure. Shit. *Think, Mari, think.* What would someone like Dane do? She had no weapons. No martial arts skills. Only her brains. They'd gotten her this far, but there was no way they'd help her in a gun fight.

In the distance she could hear another vehicle. God, please let it be Dane. Would he know she was in trouble? Would he know the pilot was dead? If he'd tried to call, he'd know something was wrong.

Her body was dragged over a rock, her head bouncing on the ground. She cried out, the sharp pain making it past her sealed lips.

"Good. Like that, did you? Lots more where it came from unless you behave yourself."

DANE SPED DOWN the empty road to the airstrip. His heart pounded and his jaw had locked a long time ago. Instinct said he'd made a mistake. A big one. Marielle was in trouble.

His foot jammed on the accelerator pedal, but the big rig wasn't going to go any faster.

He let the truck drift around the corner coming into line on the other side. They were one minute out. If he could cut that in half, he would.

The airstrip was ahead. And so was another vehicle.

"Shit."

His heart dropped at Mason's exclamation, his gaze going to the dead man on the ground close to the plane. The pilot? A fight was playing out at the other vehicle. Someone was being stuffed inside the back.

And he knew who that was.

His hand pounded on the horn even as he skidded to a stop in front of the other rig. The men were out and running before the wheels had stopped rolling. He followed, rounding the vehicle, ready for a fight.

And came to a stop.

Marielle was now standing, a black covering over her head and the asshole holding a gun to her temple.

Dane studied him. He was a stranger. Thick as a tree trunk with heavy facial features and hair. He was also a dead man, he just didn't know it.

"Back off or I kill her," the stranger snapped.

A muffled sound came from Marielle. Then she reached out and kicked her attacker.

The killer called out to her, "In case you're too stupid to understand, I'm holding a gun to your head."

But she wouldn't let up.

Dane had to admire her stubbornness even as he wished she'd cooperate – just once. It would be easier on her.

The killer slammed the gun down hard on Marielle's head.

"No," Dane whispered, frozen on the spot as Marielle wavered slightly, then sagged to her knees. The gunman let go, and she fell to the ground and didn't move again. Not the damn head again.

He didn't know how many blows she could survive before something major happened inside.

"Now, you..." he pointed the gun at Dane. "You get over here and lift her into the vehicle."

As Dane walked forward, he could feel the tension in the air. His team would jump the killer at the slightest opportunity and if Dane took a bullet, then he took a bullet – although they'd do their best to make sure it wasn't a lethal bullet. The bottom line was this guy couldn't shoot them all and he wasn't leaving.

Dane crouched down and gently picked up Marielle.

"Easy, honey," he whispered. He adjusted the weight in his arms and after a sideways look at Mason, made a jagged movement to the right behind the SUV for protection and took off at a run. The guy might have a gun, but Dane had his team.

The gun fired but it didn't hit him or Marielle. He got her to his truck and sat her in the passenger seat. He looked back to see if the fight was over. It was not only over, he could see Hawk heading into the plane. Good. Carefully Dane took the hood off Marielle and checked her head.

And heard Hawk's call. Dane paused. Not good news then.

The pilot was dead. And he'd seen a second guy dead on the ground closer to the plane.

He turned his attention back to Marielle, realizing how close they'd come to losing her.

How valuable she really was – and not just to him.

CHAPTER 12

MARIELLE OPENED HER eyes and shrieked.

"Easy, girl," said an old woman in a thick and thick gutural accent. "I'm the local doctor. I need to check your head."

But Marielle didn't believe her until Dane's head popped up over the woman.

"Oh, thank God," she muttered, trying to hold back her joy at seeing him again. "I thought I was done for last time."

"And you likely would have been if you'd gone quietly with them," he admitted. "By fighting you managed to cause him to lose time, and that was the time we needed to get to you."

"I barely remember all that happened," she said. Her gaze went to the woman. "Thank you for coming. My head is really sore."

"It's a hard head," the women said with a smile. "Now if you'd stop treating it like a ball, it might heal."

Marielle straightened slightly and looked around. She was in a hotel room of some kind. Hawk and Swede stood guard at the doorway. Dane hovered beside her and there was no sign of the others. Probably outside on watch. She hoped none of them ever left again. Shit happened when they did.

"I don't feel so good," she whispered. In fact, she was going to be sick.

She rolled over, hanging her head over the edge of the bed, and Dane shoved a garbage can under her face. She puked several times, her body shaking uncontrollably.

"See," the woman said. "You are not meant to use your head as a ball."

Right. She'd be happy to have had someone else's head banged up for a change. Hers was too damn sore as it was.

A cool cloth was pressed to her forehead. And a glass of water was placed in her hand. She drank a little bit and waited to see if it would stay down. When it appeared to rest comfortably, she drank a little more then collapsed back into bed. She was so sore.

"He dragged me across the airstrip, grabbed my phone and said they needed it too," she said in low tones. "Everything hurts."

The doctor's gaze sharpened. "They said your head was the only injury." Her hands immediately checked the rest of her.

When she was asked to roll over, Marielle went willing but cried out at the pain. Her shirt was lifted. And she heard Dane's gasp.

"What's wrong?" she cried, trying to twist and see.

"Lie still. This needs to be cleaned."

"No," Marielle said hurriedly. "I'm sure it's nothing."

"It's a road rash and filled with dirt," Dane snapped. "It has to be cleaned."

And clean it, they did. The whole time she lay with her face down in the pillow, and her body rigid.

She wanted to bawl, to fight, but knew it had to be done, and the crying just made her head hurt more. She wept into the pillow silently. By the time they were done, she was weak as a kitten and her guts churned again. There shouldn't be anything left to throw up, but her stomach was going to make sure. She shuddered, and leaning over the bed, lost the bit of water she'd drunk. Now the acid bit her throat and mouth. And the rest of her was on fire.

Dane offered her a drink of water. This time she took the drink, swished it around inside her mouth and spit it out.

Then collapsed on the pillow and closed her eyes. "You know, Dane, every time you leave me alone I end up injured and lying in bed." She frowned thinking about it, then added, "Thanks for that."

The bed creaked as he sat down beside her, his sigh heavy. "You know I'd have done anything to not have this happen to you again, right?"

"Right. But somehow it did happen. I suppose your bosses want you to dump me off somewhere in Italy now, huh? When all I want is to go home."

"You're leaving with us. We're flying out tomorrow."

"Can't fly the plane if the windshield is shot out," she said, trying to sit up so she could explain, only he pushed her back down again.

"That's why we're still here. Another plane is flying in. For us and to fix that window."

"Nice to have the whole military at your disposal."

"Hardly," he said.

"Did you find out who those men were?" she asked. "We had no warning. I heard the shot, and the next thing I knew these men had stormed the plane and grabbed me. I presume the shot took the pilot out just like that. I hope he didn't have family waiting for him at home." Tears formed at the corner of her eyes. "That's so not fair."

"Hush, you need to rest."

"He shouldn't have died." She lay there thinking of the deaths she'd been involved with this last day. "This is why I didn't want anything to do with building weapons," she whispered. "There's so much death already. And over what? They don't even have the research." God, she hoped they didn't. She hadn't heard her workplace had been broken into. But how else had Michaels planned to get his hands on her work? She hated to even think about it at this point.

"No, and they aren't going to get it either."

Just then Shadow entered. He held out a cell phone to Marielle. "This is yours – minus the tracker they had in it. At least now your calls aren't going to be traced."

Hesitantly she took it from him, her stomach knotting a little more. "A tracker?"

He nodded.

She looked to Dane, and seeing his grim look asked, "Any idea when they put it in there?"

Dane shrugged. "I was about to ask you that question."

"I have no idea. There's been no time since I arrived, but if it was done at home, then..." she looked down at the phone in her hand. "Or at work..."

She closed her eyes. "Damn. I wonder how long this has been going on." Then she remembered the email from just before the barrage on the plane.

"They sent me an image of a dead man. And my locket on his chest." She opened her email on her cell phone and showed it to them. "Supposed to have come from Michaels."

Dane took it from her and nodded. He handed it off to Shadow. "He was the shooter from an assignation. A company man. I wouldn't worry about these right now. You need to focus on getting better. It's all good."

She nodded but wasn't sure she believed him. "Promise...no, you can't." Just because she wanted it didn't mean it was fair to ask him.

"Promise what?" He leaned forward. "That you'll get home safe and sound? I'll do my best. Promise that you'll survive this? I'll do my best."

"No," she said, her voice barely audible and on the next breath asked what she really wanted to know. "Promise you won't leave me alone?"

His head lowered right to hers, she could feel his breath, the heat of his body. The surprise, yet not shocked, response to her request.

And he whispered against her ear. "I'll do my best."

And that had to be good enough. A SEALs best was damned good. She'd heard the stories of Hell Week and BUD/S training and all the over the top stories portrayed in the news about the almost secret organization that no one ever really talked about. But she was here in the middle of the team. She should be safe.

And she would be safe.

As long as Dane didn't leave her.

With that promise, she closed her eyes and drifted off to sleep. Just before going under, she felt something so soft so tender she knew she had to have imagined it, but she'd have sworn he'd kissed her.

DANE STEPPED BACK, his frown deepening as he studied Marielle's lack of color.

"She's going to be fine," the old doctor said to him.

He turned to stare at her. "How can you be sure?"

"I've been looking after people for a long time," she said. "Sure, I've lost a few over the years, but she won't be one of them. You'll need to keep an eye on her, of course, but in another day or two she'll be as right as rain."

He studied her closely, wondering if she was as full of crap as she sounded or was she seriously going on instinct and over fifty years of experience when she diagnosed Marielle's condition. They didn't have much choice in the matter. They had brought her to look at Marielle and she'd done that.

They might have to still rush Marielle to the closest hospital in the night, however, in the meantime, she could rest here with all of them hovering over her. They needed to fly out as soon as possible for her sake, but their mission wasn't over and that was major. So…this was the compromise.

He watched Mason escort the doctor out of the room. Half the team was either on guard or tracking their suspects. Shadow was on the computer tracking down the money. Someone had to know something somewhere. And that included finding out who the two dead guys from the airport were, and who they worked for. They had new strings to pull. He wanted to do something, but right now it was his turn to watch Marielle.

Dane turned to stare at her, checking on her breathing. She slept soundly. Deep. Maybe too deep. Worried, he leaned over and checked her breathing. No change since the doctor had checked her over. He was just being paranoid.

"How is she?" Mason asked. "Any change?"

"No. She's still the same."

Mason handed him a laptop. "Might as well do something

useful."

"Anyone sleeping," he asked, knowing they had to grab rest where they could.

"No. They all want revenge for our pilot. The falling out of thieves has given us two major threads to yank, so let's make good use of that opportunity."

Happily, Dane shuffled to the bottom of the bed where Marielle slept and got to work.

At least he had something he could do.

CHAPTER 13

S HE'D SPENT A lot of time in bed since meeting Dane. That was the first thought in her mind when she woke. And a lot of time fully dressed in bed. Alone. How disheartening. She glanced around to find Mason working on the laptop, Swede sitting in the corner with his head resting on his folded arms. Her gaze lit on Dane next. And she smiled. He sat head back against the wall at the foot of her bed. His eyes closed. She bet if she moved, he'd wake up in a flash. Nothing got past him.

"How are you feeling?" he asked, opening his eyes to stare at her. "Better?"

She offered him a sleepy smile. "Much better. You don't look like you got any sleep last night though."

He shrugged, his gaze never leaving her face as he carefully catalogued the change in her condition. She loved that careful attention to detail. And couldn't help but wonder if that was going to be the same attention he brought to bed? She'd love to find out. However, considering there were another half dozen men in the room with them, she didn't think they'd ever find time alone for private moments.

And there was probably a rule against it while on a mission or some such thing. She yawned, her hand coming up to cover her mouth.

"Still tired," Dane asked, frowning.

"No, not bad. Just waking up. And…" she struggled to sit up, hating the weakness in her limbs. "Waking up also means needing to go to the bathroom." Feeling embarrassed, yet knowing she had no option but to get up and go, she swung her legs over the side and sat up.

The room didn't sway. Her eyes didn't see stars. In fact, she was feeling pretty decent. Now the real test.

She made it upright, swayed slightly, righted herself as she saw Dane hop to his feet in case she needed him, and carefully made her way to the bathroom.

She could hear the men's voices after she shut the door but not the actual conversation. She used the facilities and washed her hands. After trying to straighten her hair in the mirror, she opened the door again to find Dane waiting for her.

"I'm fine."

"Good. Now back to bed with you."

With him watching her progress, she returned to the bed and sat down with her back against the headboard and her legs stretched out.

"You don't want to sleep some more?"

"No. This is good." She wanted to tell him to stop worrying but didn't think it would make any difference. "I know I was throwing up before, but right now my stomach is empty." Then she remembered the phone. "What did you find out about those men?"

Dane glanced at the others, then said in low tones, "Both were mercenaries. Neither will be missed."

That confirmed a question she hadn't wanted to ask about the fate of the man who'd dragged her across the tarmac.

Apparently they'd killed him. Then again he hadn't given them much choice. "And have we tracked who they worked for. Or who paid them to kidnap me? Or are we assuming it's the same company as the one Michaels worked for? He wouldn't share that name, by the way."

"Can't assume anything, but we tracked him to Germany. He worked for Tenesco, then ChemTech and disappeared under the radar for a while but recently popped up on Hyack's payroll so that's the assumption we're going on right now."

"Right." She wiggled to get comfortable. "Any chance of food?" she asked hopefully. "Can we go out for a meal?"

Dane shook his head. "No, but we have some here. We're keeping a low profile."

Right. So no restaurants. She wondered what that meant in this case. Army rations. She was hungry enough that might work, but she wasn't sure her stomach would agree with it.

Dane got up and headed to the small kitchenette area. There was some kind of coffee machine with a glass carafe. She smiled. Those supposedly made the best coffee of all.

He put on the kettle and opened a small fridge tucked in the cupboard below. He brought out a selection of meat and cheeses and cut several thick slabs of bread for the meal. This was her kind of meal. Now if they were on a river's edge or a mountain path with a beautiful view, she'd consider this a wonderful picnic. Sequestered inside the hotel room with men sprawled like relaxed lions all around her was a surreal setting.

A nice one. Not that the men considered her anything but a witness, maybe a victim to be looked after. And was that because they were concerned for her so she didn't end up in the enemies hands or so she was available to hand the information over to her government?

Still it was tough to consider them as friends when she didn't know them. Yet...inside she knew them. Honorable and caring at the most surprising of moments. From several of them, she'd definitely seen a male speculation. But from others there was a complete lack of interest. She'd noticed it in Mason the most. As if he was the most settled. And Hawk but she'd not been around him much. She glanced over at Swede. The big man had to be uncomfortable as he took up a large portion of the hotel room floor sleeping.

Shadow, on the other hand, was hunched over the computer so intent on what he was doing, she couldn't imagine he'd even recognize where he was.

He was well named.

Blending into his surroundings, so focused on being where he was at the moment, he was taken for granted.

Odd in a way.

She reached for a piece of sausage, only to have the same piece snatched out from under her fingers by Dane.

She gave him a mocking glare. "That was my piece."

"Too late. Around here, if you're slow you lose out."

Swede came off the floor in a smoothly coiled motion. "Did you say food? You've been eating and didn't tell anyone," he accused, walking over to observe his culinary choices.

Dane smirked. "Damn right. I wanted some myself. Not lose it all to you."

Swede brought over another plate full of food and sat down on the side of the bed. Between the three of them, she realized she felt safe. Happy. Content.

Then she spied Masters' cage. "Oh my God, I forgot about

the poor cat."

Dane snorted. "No one was allowed to forget about the cat." He pointed at Shadow, and she saw what she'd missed the first time. Masters was sprawled across Shadow's legs. Sleeping.

"Wow, it didn't take him long to settle in."

"That's because Shadow is half animal," Swede said with a straight face.

Shadow snorted. "Not likely. I'm all animal."

The others grinned.

"And yet no one offered you any of our lunch." She lifted her plate in Shadow's direction. "Please, come. I have lots."

His head shifted and he slashed his glance at her and the pieces of sausage and cheese still on her plate.

He grinned. "You aren't bigger than a cream puff. You'd better finish that so you can grow. Me, on the other hand, will go over and clean up the last of the food as soon as I set this search up." He pounded the keys several more times. "There."

He got up, carrying Masters who didn't say a word. He just watched as he was carried over and laid down on the bed close to Marielle, then scratched by all hands close enough.

"What search?" she asked when on one else did.

"I'm tracking the money the men were paid for kidnapping you."

Just as Shadow reached for food, there was a subtle knock on the door.

Everyone froze.

Then it was like an elastic had been sprung and they all moved. She'd never seen anyone move so fast. Or so quietly.

Mason slipped to the door and opened it a crack. Dane stood in front of her, blocking anyone at the door from seeing her.

Shadow was at the window, peering out. Swede, well he had a gun half hidden behind his back.

It was that gun that brought it all home for her. Someone had tried to kidnap her, and if that hadn't worked, they would have cheerfully killed her.

Since waking, that had a distant feel to it. As if it were all happening to someone else. Only it was here in her life.

She waited, her breath caught in her throat. Mason slid outside to speak with the person and the others relaxed slightly. She reached up and slipped her hand over Dane's massive arm. When he turned to look down at her, she whispered, "Has anyone checked on my mother? On my lab?"

"Your lab?" Shadow asked. "Where is your lab and what do you have there?"

She winced. "A lot of my work. I'm a grad student, so there's only so much of my work I can do outside of a professional setting."

"Name?" He parked his laptop back on his lap.

"I do much of my work at Tenesco, out of San Diego."

Getting more anxious based on his reaction, she bit her lip and waited. "I also have some work at the university." She shrugged at his hard gaze. "Not much of it, but my grad committee are all privy to what I do and where."

"So if someone wanted information, these would be the people who had it?"

She nodded. "Yes."

"Anyone else?"

Everyone stared at her. She shrugged. "I don't think so. Coworkers at Tenesco but they don't exactly think I'm doing anything of value. They've been there for decades, have multiple degrees apiece and don't really have much patience for those up and coming."

Dane grinned. "We've seen one or two like that."

Mason walked in just then. His gaze immediately went to Marielle. "How are you feeling?"

She shrugged. "Better."

"Ready to fly again?"

She brightened. "Can we go home now?"

"The plane is ready, the pilot is onboard. They are waiting for us."

That galvanized them all into action.

DANE KEPT A hand on Marielle's back as they approached the plane. The door was open and two men were on the ground checking it over. Both US Military men. According to their uniforms. But given the circumstances, Mason walked over and double-checked they were who they were supposed to be. Dane could hear the questions and answers as he walked up the small set of stairs behind Marielle. She'd been in good spirits once she realized they were on their way stateside again. She'd been professing she felt fine the whole time, and he wanted to believe her but wasn't sure. She expected a lot out of herself for repeated head injuries. He knew her recovery would be days yet. Still, she'd recover better at home and that was where they were going.

He was hoping to go see her to make sure she was healing but couldn't be sure that was a good thing. He had days off coming. And he lived in San Diego too.

He'd like to see her. If she was interested. He glanced over at her, wondering. And caught her staring back at him.

DALE MAYER

"Problems?" she asked.

He shook his head. "No, just wondering who was going to look after you when you got home."

"No one. I'm the caregiver, remember?" She glanced down at her cat carrier in her lap. Dane grinned, remembering how Masters hadn't appreciated another trip in the cage so soon. But this might be the last one for a long time. It had taken Shadow to get him in it. It was almost as if he'd explained the problem to Masters. At least after that, Masters had walked in on his own accord to the surprise of everyone around. Swede was good with animals too, but Shadow had hidden depths.

Now Masters was adjusted and complaining in his cage. He was fine as long as he was on someone's lap and not relegated to the floor. That was no place for him apparently. At least his howls had seemed to indicate that was not his position in life.

To keep the peace, they had been passing him around every hour or so.

Now in the air, Marielle appeared to have relaxed as well. She lay with Masters' cage in her arms, her head back. And appeared to be asleep.

Shadow came over, assessed the level of sleep she was in and motioned at Dane to come to the other side. Dane got up carefully but both were sleeping soundly.

"What's up?"

"One of the members on her grad committee was found beaten up on a campus path."

"Shit."

Shadow nodded. "The woman is alive but in a coma. That was followed by a break-in at the Tenesco labs. However, that was interrupted before anyone could complete the job."

"So grabbed the woman, beat the information from her, then tried to grab the research."

Dane stared out the small window in irritation. "She's not going to be safe at home, is she?"

"No."

"Then we need to keep her safe."

"We can arrange for her to go to a safe house until we figure what this is all about."

Dane considered that but realized she wasn't going to think very much about it. "Any other options?"

"We have to keep her safe so either in her space or in our space."

"Right. You know she's going to want that to be in her space?"

"She might. That doesn't mean she gets a choice."

CHAPTER 14

S HE DIDN'T GET a choice. Something she was still adjusting to when she was dropped off at a brownstone style townhome in an outlying suburban neighborhood in San Diego she had never been to and told to stay there.

"Like hell," she yelled at Dane's back as he left her inside the house and got into the big SUV. "Never," she muttered uselessly from the living room window.

She wandered the mostly empty place. There was a woman in plainclothes at the residence, likely there to keep an eye on her. She hadn't held back her opinion of what was happening to her. The woman just smiled. But she got to go home at the end of her shift. Marielle wanted to go home too. To her home. Not some cold safe house. Hell, she'd be no safer there than she would anywhere else.

Angry and tired, she plunked down on the couch and turned on the television. And bolted upright.

"Tenesco has reported a second break-in in as many days this morning. The labs have been the focus of the attacks. Tenesco, a big chemical research facility, says there is always a certain danger with these types of disturbances but that two in a row is a rarity, and they can't explain what the intruders were after."

"Well, no one asked me," Marielle snarled to the empty

room. "I could tell you a thing or two."

She dropped her head back. She had no computer with her. She had thought in her stupidity that a holiday meant a *holiday* and didn't bring it with her. She needed a way out of here. Right, a cab. She bolted upright, checked out where the woman was and snuck into the kitchen to call a cab. When they asked where to pick her up, she floundered for an answer. "Just a moment," and she walked to the front door and opened it. There was a set of brass numbers on the side. "Number 664," she said, studying the block outside. "I'm struggling to find the street name."

"When you find it, please feel free to call us back." And the operator hung up.

Pissed, Marielle turned to find the policewoman standing and watching her. She glared at her. "What street are we on?"

"Why?"

"I want to order Chinese food," she blurted without thinking then realized she could really use some food.

"Then I'll order some for you." The woman, her gaze narrow, said, "Please come back inside before you're spotted."

"Who's going to spot me," Marielle cried as she turned and went back inside. "No one even knows I've arrived back in the country."

"And that's a good thing." The woman closed the door and locked it. "Don't go back outside again, please."

"Am I a prisoner," she asked incredulously. "Surely not."

"For the moment you are not allowed to leave the safe house," she said. "I have my orders too."

Glaring at the woman for a moment and realizing she was acting like a two-year-old, Marielle turned and raced up the stairs to the room where her very much worse for wear bag and purse had been placed. And Masters.

She ran to him, listening to his plaintive cry when he saw her, and let him out of the cage. He wandered the bedroom as if looking for something until she realized he needed to go outside or to a litter box. She picked him up and carried him downstairs to the backdoor. There was a fully fenced yard so she let him go to do his business.

He stood and sniffed the air several times then walked forward several steps as if testing the ground.

She smiled.

"I asked you to stay inside," the policewoman snapped behind her.

"Masters needs a litter box for that to happen. As he didn't have that, I brought him out here. As soon as he's done, I'll take him back inside."

"I'll order one for him. Please come back in, I'll stand out here with the cat."

Marielle threw up her hands and stomped back inside. The women stood with the cat, her gaze constantly on the move. As Marielle watched her, she realized how childish she was still being. She could get through this if she had to and apparently she had to. It was to save her life.

If she were honest, the real issue wasn't that she was here but that she'd had no choice in the matter. She wanted to see her mother. She wanted to be home in her own space and she wanted to have her computer, her work. She missed it. She loved doing what she did and now felt cut off from her life. It sucked.

She also missed Dane and the others. They'd been there every moment of the last few days and now she was bereft. She liked all of them. They were good men. But she *really* liked Dane.

Even if he was arrogant and high handed. That part sucked but was kinda expected in a warrior. Unfortunately.

Masters finally appeared to be ready to walk back inside. He didn't wait for the other woman but ran lightly up the steps. Marielle opened the door for him and he came inside on his own. And meowed.

"Right. One need taken care of so now the next one, huh?" She filled a bowl with water and placed it down on the floor for him then ran upstairs to her bag where the cans of cat food were and brought them down. "We're going to have to go shopping and get you some more of these." She kept up a steady stream of conversation with the cat, happy to have him still with her. When she'd fed him and cleaned up the little mess and after finding coffee in one of the cupboards, proceeded to make a pot. She might as well be comfortable.

"I'll need my laptop if I have to stay here," she called out.

"Dane has gone to pick it up."

Marielle froze. Then a slow smile formed on her lips. He hadn't told her. But he was coming back. The smile widened into a big grin. "Oh, well I hope he grabs some clothes for me while he's there."

"I believe that was the plan."

The other woman was back on her laptop, but knowing Dane and likely the other men were returning made her much less hostile to the woman. She opened the fridge and rummaged around for food. But there wasn't much there. And no cream for her coffee either. Still, she'd been drinking it black since arriving in Germany, and she wasn't about to miss out on a cup of coffee because the amenities were lacking. While working she often drank it black.

When she was tired and stressed she preferred it with cream.

She wasn't sure what stage she was at right now.

It didn't matter as there was no cream either.

She found a pack of cookies on the counter. She took one warily. It was a standard chocolate chip variety, but she wondered how old it was. How often was the safe house used? She could really use the sugar hit.

After the first bite she realized it was relatively fresh and scarfed the rest. When she poured the cup of coffee, she decided she should be nicer and poured two. Then she grabbed up four cookies and delivered half the hoard to the other woman. "What's your name?" she asked, sitting down at the same table.

"Nancy."

"I'm Marielle." She munched on her cookie. "Are you going to be staying here with me the whole time?"

Nancy shook her head. "I'm off shift in another hour."

"Right." This was a job. She got to go home. On that note Marielle picked up her coffee. "I'm going to check what's on TV."

And she left Nancy to her work.

DANE WALKED THROUGH Marielle's classy apartment with Mason at his side. They were after her computer and any essentials she might need.

"Did you ask what she wanted from here?"

"Nope." Dane grinned at the surprised look on Mason's face. "She has no idea we're here. She wasn't going to take being shoved into a safe house alone lightly, so I figured it would be a nice surprise when I got there with her stuff."

"Ha," Mason said with a laugh. "She's going to make you pay for that."

The apartment was full of photos of days gone by and the furniture for the most part was antiques. Likely from her mother's place before she had to go into care. "Where's her mother now?"

"She's at the apartment next door with her caregiver. Shadow has gone over there."

"Right." Was that a good idea? Shadow had a way with people *when* he chose to apply it. Still, if he could reassure the two women that Marielle was okay and would be back in a couple of days, then it would make her feel better. She didn't want to lose time with her mother but neither did she want her mother worried. This was the best they could do.

He walked into her bedroom and stopped. His lady was a romantic. Long dreamy white curtains drifted from the window opened just a hair. A huge bed, he approved of that part, covered with a fluffy down comforter in a soft lemon had a half dozen pillows at the top. There was minimal furniture throughout, but what was there was good quality. He found a small suitcase in the closet and did not know what she'd want but suspected from what he'd seen her wearing she preferred comfort over fashion. He opened drawers and pulled jeans, t-shirts, a couple of long sleeved tees, and a sweater. He opened her underwear drawer and hesitated. She was a sexy romantic. Bras and silky panties lay in matched sets across the drawer bottom. He swallowed and snatched up the first five he could find. If she needed more, she'd have to do laundry like the rest of them.

He walked to her night table and opened it. There was no book or anything else special that he could see. The box of condoms in the back made his heart race and he'd have loved to toss it in the suitcase but figured that wouldn't be well received.

In the small bathroom were some toiletries. She had those that she'd travelled with, but he'd already noted she had no hairbrush so he packed one of those. He didn't know what else she might want but figured if she hadn't taken them to Europe she likely didn't need them now either.

As he walked out of the room, he found a big thick housecoat and slippers at the back of the door. He grabbed both up and threw them in. Out in the living room, he took a close look to see if there was a book she was reading or a second laptop, the first was already packed, or anything else she might want. In the kitchen he did the same perfunctory check, but there was nothing. It helped that she'd cleaned up for her trip already. Outside the apartment, he found Shadow leaving the two women next door. He had the mail keys and had collected the mail for both apartments. Dane shoved Marielle's into her bag, smiled at the two women, one who was the spitting image of Marielle if a little unfocused in her gaze, nodded to the guard standing to the one side, and with Mason and Shadow at his side, walked out.

"Let's go."

CHAPTER 15

A FTER THE COFFEE was gone, and the television failed to keep her attention, she started to pace. And pace. And pace. Then she dropped to the living room floor and started in on crunches. When fifty of those did little to stem the nervous energy flowing through her, she decided to try a different tack and set out to revitalize her body and mind with yoga. She was a little rusty, but her body thrived on the positions. When she finally settled into a final resting pose, her mind was calm and her body at peace.

Until she looked up and saw Dane in the doorway.

Her heart exploded as she raced toward him. She never thought twice about throwing herself into his arms, and as his opened and closed tightly around her, she figured it was the right thing to do. He twirled her around then set her on her feet to eye her critically.

"I'm fine."

"You look great," he admitted with a big grin. "Nice to see. No headache? No lingering pain?"

"No. I've been hyper and having trouble settling but the yoga helped."

Then she spied her suitcase. "You brought my clothes." She laughed and grabbed the bag to lug upstairs, but he grabbed it out of her hand.

"I'd say hi," Mason called from behind her, "but apparently the suitcase has more importance than the other people in your life."

She gasped, spun and launched herself into his arms.

He chuckled and gave her a big hug.

"I'm so sorry. I'm so happy to see you. Of course if you'd been here earlier I might have been more likely to have slugged you instead." She grinned. "But time and distance and understanding..."

"And a suitcase?" He smirked.

Swede's head popped up behind Mason. "Geesh and I thought I'd get a little appreciation for bringing your laptop."

"Oh my laptop," she cried. Mason stepped aside in time for her to hug the big man and snatch the laptop out of his hands. "I've been wanting this all day." She shot them a guilty look and added, "Actually all week. I use my phone for most things, but it's not the same."

Swede still had his arm around her when Shadow walked up and tilted her chin so he could check her head wound.

She chuckled. "A couple of hours ago I figured I was all alone, and you guys had dumped me forever."

"Never," he dropped a kiss on her cheek. "Glad to see you looking so much better."

Hawk was the last one inside. He lifted the two bags he carried and asked her, "Hungry? I believe someone mentioned food."

The aroma hit her first.

"Chinese?" He was hugged with the same fervor that the others had received. Laughing and talking, they all moved into the kitchen where she dug out plates for everyone. Dane returned to find all the chairs full and everyone busy scarfing food.

The others took one look and grinned at his sour expression.

"Sorry you were too late," Hawk said.

"We can make room for you," Marielle said, standing up and trying to figure out how. The men completely dwarfed the small room, taking up the whole kitchen. "Somehow…" but her voice trailed off.

"I have a solution to that," Dane said. He quickly took Marielle's spot and tugged her down onto his lap. Then he grabbed the last plate and dumped food onto it. With the last fork, he shifted her slightly to the side, picked up his plate and proceeded to eat.

Marielle wasn't too sure how to handle the new situation. She hadn't considered this option, but as a solution, it worked for her. And she quickly lost her sense of discomfort as everyone accepted the situation as normal.

It was far from normal, but if this was the "new normal," she was more than happy with it.

They polished off all the Chinese food with the men looking at the empty containers with sad expressions. She laughed. "If someone puts on coffee, I'll share the pack of cookies I found today."

There was a mad scramble as everyone raced to clean up and get coffee on. When she brought the package over, it lasted about three seconds.

"Boy, you guys can eat."

Swede snorted. "Hasn't been any food to eat yet." He stretched up his fingers to spread across the ceiling. "Down home we'd eat real food. Good stuff there."

"Where's there?" She looked at him as she walked into the living room with a cup of coffee. She knew by the time everyone got a cup the last person was going to have to put on a new pot, and she wasn't going to be it. "I presume Sweden."

"Hell no. I'm from Denmark."

She shook her head. "That makes no sense." She motioned to Dane. "I'd have thought he was from Denmark with his name and you from Sweden from your name."

"Nicknames aren't from location," Dane explained as he sprawled across the love seat. "He's got a great reason for his nickname, right Swede?"

"Says you. If there were some here and now, I'd make that nickname stick all over again."

Mason laughed. "Marielle, he's called Swede for winning at a Swedish meatball eating contest we held back when we were still in training."

"Eating meatballs? I'm scared to ask, how many did you eat?"

He shrugged. "Two hundred twenty-four."

She blinked. "In one sitting?"

He nodded.

"Not possible."

Swede laughed. "Hell, Dane here ate over two hundred. Shadow came in not far behind."

"And Hawk and Mason, how did they do?"

"Hawk counted and Mason timed."

"I'd have loved to see that." And she would have. The men were a great bunch of guys. She walked over to the couch but with no place to set her coffee down, she was at a loss as to where to put it.

"Give it to me," Dane said, holding out his hand. He placed it on the coffee table in front of him. Then tugged her down beside him, her back to the window. "Then if you want a drink you can reach from here."

She smiled. He looked like a lazy cat. And the grin on his face just added to his Cheshire appearance.

Sitting as she was, she was tucked up against his side, and almost wrapped in a Dane blanket as he curled around her giving her enough room to sit but with himself taking the rest of the available space.

The rest of the men had all taken up spots that ranged from the other couch to the floor to Shadow who'd grabbed a kitchen chair and was sitting on the hearth and using the kitchen chair to work on his laptop.

She had no idea what he was doing now. She thought about asking but wasn't sure she wanted to bring up the topic. It was peaceful here. Work was going to change that energy. Mason turned on the television and checked the news stations for updates.

When there was talk of a serial killer on the loose, he changed it. When there was talk of an uprising in a local prison, he changed it. When a rapist got off with less than six months for his crimes, he changed it. But not fast enough.

"Is there ever anything nice on the news," she cried. "Or happy?"

"No. That's not why the news is on."

"And that's why I don't know any women who watch the news. It's depressing. You'd never go outside if you listened to all the crazy stories." She shivered and rubbed her arms.

"Easy. You're safe here, and hopefully you've met all the crazies you're ever going to meet," Dane said. He reached out and grabbed her hand. "It's not all bad news."

She nodded, not convinced, but willing to let him make her feel better. She leaned forward for her cup of coffee when an odd sound rang out. She was slammed to the floor, Dane's big body covering hers.

"What happened?" she cried out.

"Someone just shot at you."

AND THAT WAS why she shouldn't be at a safe house. Like who determined it was safe? Much better to blend into the urban jungle. This was too damn predictable.

He held Marielle beneath him while his team scattered. He never heard a door open but knew his men were already searching outside for answers. The vehicle had taken off in a scream of tires and backfires. Interesting that they used an obvious vehicle. Then again like the other attempts, they'd probably tried to change tactics and hired a local thug. Drive by shootings were very hands off. Of course, not knowing if there was someone even now trying to sneak in, he'd hold judgment. But first he had to get Marielle to a safe place. Too bad there wasn't a garage with a parked vehicle in it. It would be easier to sneak her out that way.

"Go," she whispered. "Go find this bastard. Don't worry about me."

He snorted. "Like hell." He lifted his weight up off her incredibly soft body and hauled her up with him. Keeping low, he led her through the living room into the kitchen, with her hidden by his body, he searched the gloom around the outside of the house. Mason's call through the window told him it was safe. He gave an answering call.

Mason entered silently. He gave Dane a hard look, saw Marielle tucked behind him and gave a curt nod. "Nothing outside around the house."

"Drive by?"

"Not random, targeted."

Dane nodded. "Ready to leave?"

Mason snorted. "Past ready."

The others filtered in slowly. Shadow came up behind them. "I've already loaded her bags up."

"Masters?" Marielle asked.

Shadow grinned. "Yeah, he's as happy to leave as we are."

"Let's move." Dane shuffled Marielle ahead of him and out into the night. She'd barely spoken since the shooting but seemed as willing as the rest of them to leave. They couldn't stay here now that the location was compromised and how that happened he'd take great pleasure in finding out. The local policewoman had left when they'd arrived.

They were in the vehicles and on the road in minutes. Riding convoy style they ran through several practiced maneuvers to make sure no one was tailing them.

Dane headed straight to a house they'd used before. They were lucky enough to have several at their disposal that they'd been forced to use at odd times. Never more than once in a year and with any luck never twice at the same place in a row. But shit happened and even SEALs needed a place to lay low.

By the time he pulled into the garage in the back of the large acreage and turned off the engine, Marielle was asleep. Shadow had been riding shotgun. He unloaded Marielle's bags and

Masters and went ahead of them. Dane walked around the vehicle, opened the passenger door and carefully lifted her out. Using his hip, he closed the door and walked into the house. It was set back on the lot and surrounded by huge trees. And was empty as they'd expected. Shadow had left the door open and was doing a quick search of the premises.

Dane carried Marielle upstairs to the back bedroom that had a deck with a set of stairs leading to the backyard. Easy escape for them if trouble came calling and if it came calling up that set of stairs then they'd get a surprise – him. He had no intention of leaving her here alone.

He lay her down on the covers and flipped the spare material over top of her.

She never woke.

Needing to make sure, he watched her steady slow breathing. She had to be still affected by her injuries. And she was exhausted.

And so damn innocent. He stroked a finger down her cheek.

"Sleep," he whispered. "You're safe."

She murmured something unintelligible and curled deeper into the covers.

Dane took up a position at the windows. A shadow slipped through the trees. One he recognized. Shadow on patrol. That meant the house was empty and he was out checking on the night.

Dane wanted to go downstairs but wasn't going to leave Marielle alone. Leaving the door open, he checked the hallway to see what else was upstairs. Two more bedrooms. Two more bathrooms. Several closets, all empty. He returned to Marielle's bedroom and slipped out on the deck, leaving the door open.

He waited for the morning to come.

CHAPTER 16

S HE WOKE TO fresh air wafting over her, and sunlight, light airy morning sunlight dappling across her bed. She stretched and yawned. She studied the ceiling above her and frowned. This wasn't the room she'd been in yesterday? Then again she hadn't been in it very long. She rolled over and looked at the rest of the room. And bolted upright.

The old room didn't have a deck or an open door. Nor did it have this luxurious decor. This was a beautiful house. She slipped off the bed and stared down. She was fully dressed. Only her shoes were off, and they'd been placed on the floor beside her. The white carpet wasn't conducive to wearing shoes. An open door on the other side revealed a small bathroom. She made her way over and stopped in surprise. There was nothing small about this bathroom. Like the bedroom, it was stunning in both opulence and classiness. It was almost a shame to mar the beauty by using the facilities. But it had been a long night. Afterwards she washed her hands and face and looked longingly at the shower. Except there was no way she was stripping down in a strange house at this point. Was she a prisoner? Or were the guys here?

Time to find out. She opened the door and stepped out.

The room was still empty. She walked across to the deck

door and peered out. Dane sat there watching her. She glanced back at the bedroom and realized he'd known the moment she woke up.

For some reason that didn't sound creepy to her. Instead it reassured her he was taking such great care.

Then she remembered the bullets firing into the house. And the wild escape. She had no recollection of reaching this destination.

"Good morning," he said, his eyes bright, assessing. "How did you sleep?"

"Considering I don't remember going to sleep," she said, "I slept well."

She sat down on the deck chair beside him. "Thank you for looking after me."

His lips quirked, making her heart race.

"You're welcome."

"What are we doing here?" She thought she'd done well to not immediately ask a million questions that were bubbling up. She was surprisingly calm about the whole thing.

"A new safe house."

She laughed. "We could have come here first, it's beautiful."

"Had to do it as ordered." His voice hardened. "Until the safe house was compromised."

"I gather you weren't happy about the first safe house?"

He shrugged. "It is what it was. I often disagree with authority." His big grin flashed white. "It's why I make a great SEAL. Not hampered by the same rules as everyone else."

She laughed. "I can see that. And you do make a great SEAL. I wouldn't be here if it weren't for you." She pondered that then added in a serious voice, her hand reaching across to his beefy forearm, "I do appreciate all you've done for me, so thank you." She leaned across and kissed his cheek.

At the last moment he turned and her lips landed on his mouth. He reached up with his free hand and held her head so he could kiss her properly. By the time he released her, she sagged back into her chair a happy boneless jelly mold.

"You're welcome," he said, a smirk on his face.

She glared at him. "You did that on purpose."

"Did what?" He feigned innocence. "You kissed me."

She snorted. "I started to kiss you. But you ended up kissing me."

"No," he corrected, his eyes dancing with the devil, "I kissed you back."

She sighed. "This is a ridiculous conversation."

"But fun."

She laughed. "True. So now that I'm awake, my body is screaming for food."

"Not caffeine? I figured that would be the first requirement."

"They go together," she admitted. "And I'd love both."

"Good, then I arrived at the right time, so it's me you will appreciate this morning," Swede said as he walked in with two big mugs in his hands.

"Oh." She hopped up and walked over to him. "I so appreciate you."

"The same as you appreciate this big idiot," he asked hopefully, a twinkle in his eyes.

Heat washed over her face as she realized he'd seen the kiss. "Absolutely," she lied with a grin and gave him a chaste kiss on the cheek.

When he laughed and made no move to take advantage of

her, she turned back to Dane, the coffee in her hand, and said, "See, he's a gentleman."

"No, he just knows I'd pound him into the ground if he did more."

She gasped and turned to Swede whose grin widened as he said, "You could try."

Dane laughed. He kicked his legs back and stretched out. "If you're here to look after sleeping beauty, I'm going to grab five." And he closed his eyes.

Marielle watched in surprise as he visibly relaxed in front of her to the point that deep relaxed breathing slid out of his chest in regular rhythms in no time. She scooted her chair over to Swede in order to not wake Dane while talking.

"Can you sleep like that," she asked in a low voice. "So fast?"

He nodded. "We learned to catch rest where and when we can. We've been running sentry duties all night to keep watch and when our watch is over we power nap until it's time to wake up again."

"Amazing." And so damn helpful. She could learn a lot from these guys.

HE WOKE ALONE. He lay still for a long moment letting his body adapt. Awareness of his surroundings was instant. His instincts were calm, no danger approached. In fact, it was a lazy summer day. He opened his eyes loving the blue sky and light breeze. A beautiful day. And not a day to die.

With a light energy burst he surged upwards and walked the small deck, shaking out his limbs. His gaze found Hawk in position. He gave him a hand signal and watched the returning gesture. All okay. Then he'd expected that. No one should know about this place.

And having arrived under the cover of darkness with only one vehicle on the premises, no one could know how many men were on site.

Just the way they liked it. The element of surprise was everything.

Inside the bedroom he found Marielle's bed made and her original travel bag beside the bag he'd brought her lying on the bed, but closed and ready to go at a moment's notice. Smart girl. His gaze lingered on the huge bed wishing for a few nights alone with just her and away from the danger that surrounded her. She was someone he admired. And would love to get to know better. Hell, he'd love to bed her and hope that would take the fascination away.

It always had before.

This time he didn't think it would. She was something different. Right from the first moment she'd seen him in the garden in Germany he'd been fascinated. That she'd recognized him for what he was and had come running to him when she'd been in trouble – yeah, that said a lot about her.

Now he could only hope they had a future to figure out just what this craziness between them was all about.

Noises drifted up from downstairs. They were in the kitchen. From the aroma floating his way, he suspected brunch was in the offing.

Just in time. His stomach was trying to eat its way out.

He stopped at the doorway, surveyed the backyard, the trees and the outside of the house. Satisfied that all was as it should be, he made his way to the kitchen.

And Marielle.

CHAPTER 17

MARIELLE KNEW THE minute Dane woke up. Like an instinctive jolt to her psyche. By the time he walked into the kitchen her nerves were alive and singing. Damn, this man moved her in ways she'd never known.

She smiled at him as he walked in and laughed. "Good morning, sleepyhead. Did you have a nice nap?"

The snigger started behind her. And wrapped all around the room.

Mason patted the seat beside him. "Come sit young'un. Do you feel better now?"

Shadow guffawed. Dane walked right up to Marielle, reached down, picked her up and kissed her – thoroughly. Then put her back on her feet. She grabbed for the counter as her body sagged.

Masculine satisfaction shone on his face as he walked to the seat beside Mason and said, "I had a great nap – how about you?"

The men grinned and dove in as Marielle recovered enough to bring over the pan full of sausages to add to the huge bowl of scrambled eggs Shadow had whipped up.

She sat down beside Dane and served herself a scoop of eggs and a sausage. As soon as she forked up her first bite, a second sausage and a second serving of eggs landed on her plate. Dane calmly ignored her gasp, saying, "Eat. You don't know when we'll get the next meal."

A horrible reminder that this wasn't a holiday and wasn't a group of friends enjoying brunch.

"Right." Aware of the darker mood falling on the table but realizing it was necessary, she asked, "What are we doing now?"

"Hiding," Mason said.

Her movements slowed. "What good does that do?" she asked in confusion.

"Keeps you alive."

"But for how long," she cried. "We have to go after these guys."

"And who are you going to go after?" Mason asked quietly. "We're looking for the guys who killed the professor."

She stared at him.

"And if you have anyone to suggest we take a closer look at, then speak up so we can hunt them in cyberspace."

She nodded, feeling better, and of course they were working on it. It wasn't like they could sit here and babysit her for the rest of her life. Although she'd love that.

"Speaking of your Ph.D. committee, did anyone there help you get the position at Tenesco?" Dane asked.

"No, I got that job through Professor Michaels. His buddy worked there for years and was looking for a new grad student."

Silence.

She cut a slice of sausage and popped it into her mouth. Then realized it was too silent.

"What?" she asked as soon as she swallowed her mouthful.

"Do you know other people that were friends of Michaels?" Shadow asked, his laptop now suddenly on the table beside him.

"James. Dr. Dennis James, who was killed in a car accident,

was a good friend," she said around a mouthful of food. "He died a few months back."

More silence.

"Damn," Mason said. "Why did we not ask you about his associates before?"

She shrugged. "What about who knows him at Tenesco, like Hudson? Or Dr. Hoerner, the guy who hired me, and his German associates. Tenesco has an agreement with a large chemical company in Germany. And another in China."

Breakfast was forgotten as more laptops appeared and notepads came out.

Suddenly the questions shot her direction rapid fire.

She answered as fast as she could. Some she had only a vague idea and others were right there in her brain.

A half hour later she was exhausted from the instant brain drain, and the intensity of the questions. She'd no idea that she had so much information stuck in there. By the time the questions wound down, the men were buried either on the phones or on their laptops or in Mason's case, maps. And what he could be looking at she had no idea.

Feeling tired and needing something else to do, she stood up and started cleaning off the table. All the dishes had been shoved to the center. She moved them over to the sink and washed them up quickly. Then set up coffee. She kept checking on the men, but they were deeply involved in their research.

Good. After she had cleaned up, she walked into the living room and grabbed up her laptop. Turning it on, she brought up her email and sorted through it. She'd lost her phone somewhere along the way and when she'd found it, she'd been too ill to care about her emails. Although she'd missed it initially, she'd found a certain freedom in being disconnected. Now she had hundreds of emails to catch up on. Although as she went through the bulk of them, the delete button was used heavily. Several emails were from other students. She answered the ones she could and marked the ones she'd need to do later.

By the time she'd gone through all the ones piled up, she checked for incoming emails and watched as three more downloaded.

Two she deleted without looking and then clicked open the third.

She hit the ground running before her eyes had truly seen or her mind truly understood what she was looking at.

"Dane!" she cried.

She was in the kitchen as the men bolted to their feet.

She handed over her laptop and cried, "Look."

DANE STARED AT the laptop, his mind still adjusting from the shock of her cry and believing she was in trouble to the image of a dead man staring up at him.

Narrow eyed he stared at the email address and the simple message.

"You're next," he read aloud.

The others crowded around behind him. He looked over the top of the screen at Marielle. "Do you know this man?"

She was slowly going to pieces now that the visual threat had shown up. She nodded. "Dr. Hudson. He works at Tenesco. One of the arrogant chemists." Tears came to her eyes. "Oh my God," she cried. "I shouldn't say that. He's dead. The poor man is dead."

There was no doubt about that as the man's throat appeared to have been cut. He was dressed in a lab coat and showed signs of torture. His fingers were skinned and there appeared to be burn marks on the back of his hands. Several fingers were twisted the wrong way.

"Would he have any idea about the research you are doing?"

"Not access to it, I don't think," she said, her arms tightly crossed over her chest. "But he's the head of the lab. I don't know how their security or password system runs. Anyone at Tenesco could in theory have access. I'm low on the company ladder. I imagine all the chemists and department heads above me could."

"Is there a reason why he'd be chosen to have information about your project?"

She whitened. "He publicly claims credit for everyone else's work. So he probably said something to the wrong person. But even he doesn't know all I'm doing."

"Does anyone?"

"No–" she stopped herself in mid thought. "Professor Michaels. He knew a lot of it."

"And we've already heard all these names? Any others?" Shadow asked.

"No, I gave them to you already." She sat back down at the kitchen chair. "I need to contact Candice. She's going to be devastated."

"His wife?"

She shook her head. "No, the admin. She runs the department really. But hasn't got the title. It's typical of many departments. The person who keeps it running is the one with the real power."

"And we've never heard of Candice, why?" Shadow had an affronted tone to his voice. "She could be key."

Marielle laughed at the idea. "No. She's a small Asian lady who runs that place like a military barracks."

"Asian," Mason said quietly. "Does she have any connection to the other companies?"

"No," she said. "Candice is an administrator. She was a chemist trained in another country but couldn't get recognition for her degree over here and when her husband got a good job she gave up on the idea and started at the company as an admin. Now because of the degree, she's the perfect person to run the department."

"What's her temperament like?" Shadow asked.

"Uhm." Marielle winced. "I'm afraid she's a bit acerbic. I figured she'd been in the job too long. She knows everyone and hates a lot of them."

"We'll go and talk with her," Shadow said. "See if she'll tell us anything."

"She won't," Marielle said. "She's not very friendly."

"You don't like her?"

"She's efficient but not easy to get along with. However, she loved Dr. Hudson. That's why I know she'll be devastated."

"Will she or could she have been so angry that she had something to do with his death?"

She shook her head. "No, I don't think so."

After several more minutes of questions, Mason and Shadow got up and slipped out the back. If she hadn't been watching them, she wouldn't have realized they were going, they moved so quietly. Leaving her alone with Dane.

CHAPTER 18

"I PRESUME THEY have gone to talk to her?"

"And check out other leads," Dane said.

"And what do we do while they're gone?"

"You are supposed to heal. Rest, relax and get better."

She snorted. "So everyone else gets to do something useful, and I get to lie here and do nothing." She threw her hands up in the air. "I hate that. I want something to do. Something proactive. I hate waiting and I hate being a victim."

"But you like being alive and that's the point we're at right now. Keeping you alive."

"But they are trying to kill me – why? If they wanted what I know then they would try to kidnap me. If they have my research they don't need me. And they wouldn't need to kill me."

"Unless they figure that Michaels told you something about who they are, and so they are cleaning up."

She stared at him wordlessly. "Just because of that? Do people kill over such little things?"

"You put their whole organization at risk. Imagine a big company selling chemical warfare to our enemies."

She paled. "That's terrible. I don't want my research to be involved in something like that," she cried. "That's not what I'm trying to do."

"But it's what is happening, so we have to nip it in the bud before that is the end result."

He stood up and tugged her into his arms. "We can't think about what you would have preferred to have happened but rather deal with what *is* happening."

She snuggled in close then reared back to look up at him. "We have to stop this."

"We are working on it."

"No, let's go to the company and destroy my research."

"There's a couple of things wrong with that idea. First, I doubt you own it. Second, there will be copies of it, third, it's likely already been stolen and fourth, we need to know what it might all be so that our people can develop some type of defense against it." He pulled her in tight and just held her. "Remember," he said. "It's not your fault."

"And yet it feels like I'm to blame."

"Because of your research?"

She nodded.

"But this isn't what you planned to do. It happened. In many ways, this discovery could be brilliant," he admitted. "Particularly if used against our enemies. Like anything, we wouldn't want it turned against us, so we need to know the details so we can come up with a line of defense against it."

"Or I destroy it completely," she said in a small voice. "Then no one needs to get hurt."

He hugged her close. "We should be so lucky to live in a world without war. I could hope that it would happen in my lifetime – at least in my children's lifetime."

At the word children, she froze, then lifted her head. "Do you have children?"

"No." He laughed. "But maybe one day I will."

"Yeah, me too."

She lay her head against his chest, appreciating the moment. There'd been so few lately.

"Now considering that you've given us several leads, I need to track some of them down." He looked around. "Maybe in the kitchen. Where are you going to be? I can work anywhere, so pick a room and I'll move with you."

"The table here is fine." She stepped back and gathered up her laptop and workbooks and set up on one end of the table. "I'll work here." As she brought up her work, he shifted so he took over the other side of the table. Settled, she got down to refreshing her mind on where she'd finished on her research paper. There were several work oriented emails. Thankfully there were no other nasty ones. She could tell from the way Dane stared at her as she got started that he was expecting something less than pleasant. She smiled up at him. "Just the normal emails."

"Good." He disappeared into his work.

She spent a pleasant hour working on her paper until Hawk walked in the door.

He sniffed the air. "I missed breakfast, didn't I?"

"You did," Dane said from behind his computer. "But there are cold sausages in the fridge beside the eggs."

Surprised, she watched Hawk prepare a hefty breakfast for himself. He caught her looking at him at one point and smiled curiously at her. "What's the matter?"

"I was surprised you are cooking," she admitted. "But I shouldn't be. You are all so damn capable it's scary."

"How can capable be scary?" Hawk scoffed. "It should make

you feel better to know we can handle many situations."

"Oh it does," she teased. "It makes you guys ideal men."

"Hawk is, but he's taken now," Dane said. "Our last set of days off ended up being worse than many of our missions, but the end result is he found someone special. Isn't that right, Hawk?"

"It is," Hawk said cheerfully. "Talk about a life event."

"Really, you guys have long-term partners?"

Both men looked at her. She flushed. "Sorry, I just figured that with the stress and danger you'd avoid long-term relationships. Not that you couldn't have them or wouldn't have them just…" she stopped and shrugged, "I'm an idiot…"

"Not at all," Hawk said gently. "It *is* an issue with us. Many don't do well married. Some military wives can't handle the stress and uncertainty of sending their men off to war every day. Same goes for law enforcement of all kinds. It's a problem. However, there are many successful marriages. Special women who can handle it. I lucked out."

"And so did Mason," Dane said quietly. "He's been the leader in this area."

"Really?" She thought about the man and smiled. "Makes sense."

Dane looked at her suspiciously. "What makes sense?"

"That Mason is in a committed relationship. There isn't the same roaming eye on him that there is in many of the other men. He's not only in a relationship, he's happy to be with *her*."

The other two men nodded. "It's an ideal situation, but so few military men manage to get it."

"And I'm keeping you from her," she said softly. "I'm sorry."

"Don't be. It's the job. And if it wasn't you, it would be

something or someone else. She knows it and so do I."

"Still..." she felt odd realizing that as much as she really liked these men they all had lives she wasn't a part of. Lives they could go to when the job was done. She needed the reminder. Right now she was a job to them.

And they would get to go home at some time when the "job" was over.

They were nice to have as friends and Dane...well she'd love to have him as more than a friend but it wasn't likely to happen. She cast a look in his direction and found him staring at her.

She raised an eyebrow in question, but he shrugged and went back to working on his laptop.

She understood how he felt. There was no understanding or explaining this inexplicable draw to each other. Attraction was one thing. This...was something else. She wondered at Hawk and Mason and their relationships. What were the women like? Would she like them? She had so few friends and most were men. She'd love to have a core group of women friends.

So far it hadn't happened. There were a few at work but they were older. Less on the friendly side. She'd thought she'd make more friends at the university but had found that studies had completely taken up most of her time and she'd not been a party animal. That hadn't left much opportunity or time to meet other women. Men were easier to be friends with. And she'd naturally gravitated toward the men, so it had been an easy choice.

Now at her age, she found herself wishing for more women in her life.

DANE DRILLED THROUGH the layers of hierarchy in Tenesco's

history. The company had connections. Did they know what their people were doing? Or were they actively requiring this type of behavior, as the company itself was involved in things it shouldn't be? He hadn't been able to find anything odd on the surface of course, and even now as he checked deeper into their history and the roots of the company, nothing was raising red flags. Except it was involved in a major takeover a few years ago. The previous board of directors had been fired and the new company replaced every one of the top management personnel. He was still checking the old versus the new. He asked Marielle about it.

"Oh, that's right. I'd worked there the summer before I went to university over the winter and went back early spring and all the upper management staff were gone. Not that I have much to do with any of them, but there'd been a lot of talk. The new owners were taking the company in a new direction. Although I have no idea what that meant. There was a lot of talk as people worried about their jobs for months then as a big boom wasn't lowered, they eased up. I'm not sure I ever met anyone in the new management team. Hudson wasn't happy with the changes though and was fairly voluble about it in private. He was always perfect when the company bosses wandered the floor but wouldn't say anything nice about them later."

"It happens that way sometimes. Mergers and takeovers are not always welcome, and people often lose their jobs in the shuffle."

"Several jobs were lost and several people were ugly about it, but it's not like they are going to steal information from the company as a way to pay it back for losing their job," she protested lightly.

Dane just stared at her. "That's exactly what they do."

"Really?" Her shoulders sagged and she muttered, "Why are people so…much like people?"

"You are just living in a world full of sunshine and rainbows."

Silence at the table had him looking up at her. Had he upset her? "What?"

"I *was* living in a world like that," she said. "But I'm not anymore."

Hawk brought his plate to the table, changing the tone of the conversation.

"Did you see anything out there, Hawk?" she asked.

He shook his head. "Peaceful and calm. Sunshine and rainbows all the way." And he grinned at her.

She laughed. Dane shook his head.

The peaceful camaraderie set the tone for the rest of the afternoon.

CHAPTER 19

S HE CLOSED HER books and yawned. "I hardly did anything but I'm tired already." She stacked up her books and set them at the back of the table. "I think I should go to the company and get the rest of my stuff."

He lifted his head from his laptop and said, "I thought you said it was all on the servers."

"It is there too but my own stuff is on my keys."

"Who would know this?"

"No idea. It's not like I've been hiding my work all these years. They'd have seen me use keys over time. Stuff I was bringing back and forth to work on at home. Backups. Copies for presentations."

"But all the work is on the servers at the company as well?"

She nodded. "We have a login to the server and like any company they have security safeguards in place."

"But..." He waited.

"I work on my laptop a lot. And work from home even more so I needed a way to carry the information back and forth." She shrugged. "That's not new or different."

"Not if this research is important and people are trying to get it. Then it's a case of needing to know how many copies of the material there are."

"Two. The servers and my key."

"And your laptop?"

"Not really. Bits and pieces I suppose but I work off the key."

"And yet you don't have your key with you."

She flushed. "Right. I switched to cloud storage a little while ago."

He just stared at her. "So you don't need the key anymore?"

She threw up her hands. "Hey, it's got some stuff on it I need, so I usually have all of it available just in case. I've been transferring some to cloud storage, but I'm only using the free space and it's not very big so the key, cloud, laptop and work."

"That doesn't sound like a very good system."

"It's not, but I was a student and viewing my work more along the lines of schoolwork not chemical warfare," she snapped. "I'd be happy to change this and put it all on the cloud and the server but that means going to the lab." She brightened. "That's actually a really good idea."

"No, it's not."

"Yes it is. I'll be able to grab my other books I need too," she waved a hand at the stack on the table. "I didn't bring home everything I wanted last time so could use a couple more of my textbooks."

"I'm not sure you showing up at the company is a good idea at all," he admitted. "It might trigger another attack."

"That would mean people are watching Tenesco, so if that's the case, what about the fate of the other people who work there? Are they in danger too?" She shook her head, sending her hair flying. "I can't have that on my conscious too."

She stood up. "That's enough. Let's go to my company, I

can grab the stuff I need and you'll be able to see what the layout and system is like. It's not chemical warfare there."

"If not there," he said standing up, "then how about at a sister site? Where different work is carried out but still sits under the same umbrella corporation."

"I hate the sound of any of it. I don't want to believe the company I've been working for is involved in anything so horrible."

"You work in chemistry. What did you think they worked on?"

"They develop industrial chemicals," she said in a harsh tone. "Not weapons."

Hawk's head continued to flip from one side to the other as he listened to the conversation and the two glaring adversaries. Marielle wanted to comment but figured it would make things worse. She slumped back down. "Whatever."

Dane sat down opposite her.

Hawk smirked. Marielle caught the look and frowned at him. "What are you smiling about?"

"You two." He got up from the table and walked to the sink where he washed his dishes. "Lots of energy between you two."

"So? He's irritating as hell." When Hawk laughed she frowned. "Whatever."

"Let's go to Tenesco," Dane said.

She brightened. "Really?"

Dane nodded. "You're not going to rest until you can grab your stuff."

"Well, it is my work," she said apologetically. She bounced toward the doorway. "Let me grab my jacket."

"IS THAT WISE?" Hawk asked. "The reason we're safe here is no one knows where she is."

"I know but Tenesco is where it's at."

"But not locally. It's going to be in Germany or China most likely."

"I hear you. Need to know where first." Dane looked at the doorway to make sure she wasn't listening in. "Also, she seems to think no one there is looking at her research, not her coworkers, friends, etc. We know better. There are always people looking to climb that ladder."

"True." Hawk stared out the window. "Even when we're not on duty we're on duty. The rest of the world, however…"

"Exactly."

"I'm not sure we're heading in the right direction on this."

"No, quite possibly we aren't. But we have to figure it out soon. She's getting antsy and won't stay like this for long."

"I wouldn't either. But I'd be going after the enemies not waiting for them to come after me."

"But I can't do that," Marielle said from the doorway. "I wish I could. But with Michaels gone, and the head of my chemistry department at work gone, I'm not a fool. I can't go after a nameless killer."

Dane walked over to her. "You can't, but that doesn't mean we can't."

She nodded but didn't look convinced. "What I can do is my work."

"Let's go. We'll go to your lab and grab your stuff." As she turned and walked to the front door, Dane nodded to Hawk. "At least this way, the work might not fall into anyone else's hands."

"I'll be watching your back."

"Good. Let's hope it's a quick trip. We should be back here in just over an hour."

CHAPTER 20

THE DRIVE TO the lab where she'd spent so much of her last few years took longer than she expected. It took ten minutes of driving time alone for her to understand where she was in the city. She knew she'd never make it back on her own. That gave her a weird feeling of isolation.

Outside in the parking lot, she stared around the massive grounds. So much had happened since she'd been here that she couldn't imagine how untouched it looked. There'd been several break-ins and a death, yet the immaculate grounds were the same. The building looked the same. If any physical damage had been done, it wasn't obvious anymore. She walked up the long sidewalk to the front door. The doors were closed. She used her key card to pull it open and walked into the front reception.

It was empty.

No one in the expansive seating area and no one behind the desk. She took a left turn, opened the steel door with her key card and headed down the long stairwell to where the labs were. And her locker. As they walked the long hallway, she couldn't help noticing that the place appeared empty of staff. She hadn't seen anyone at the front desk. And so far the other offices were closed and lights off. Then she realized what the problem was. "What day of the week is it?"

"Saturday."

She smiled. "Right. There wouldn't be anyone here normally on a Saturday."

"No one?"

"Not usually."

"But you were allowed to be here on weekends?" his voice sounded odd.

"I think I've only been here once on a weekend," she admitted. "And that was to pick up work."

"So you don't know if people are here or not?" he said it in such a matter of fact voice she didn't take offense. Besides, she didn't really know. She hadn't been in on a weekend lately so didn't know and the one time she had come in she'd been asked about it on Monday.

"I guess." She shrugged. "They are watching us now on camera so I'll get questioned on Monday."

"That would be normal of any company. I'm surprised you didn't have to sign in first as you entered."

"The cards replaced the sign-in requirement as they are coded individually for each person and are needed at each level and door. So much safer."

"Unless you're dead and the cards can be used by someone else."

"Great, thanks for the reminder. Besides, they might get in with my card, but they still would be on camera."

She finally made it to her level and walked out onto the floor. On the left side were small labs with large glass observation walls. On the right were small offices.

At the third office she pulled out her key and opened the door.

"Damn it," she cried. "I was hoping no one had been in here." She stared at her simple bare room with papers strewn on the floor, drawers pulled out and dumped, and her cup tossed to the ground. She placed her laptop down on the desk and turned it on. "I don't keep anything here on purpose."

"And that could be why it was dumped like this – temper."

"Makes no sense. Everything is stored on the server."

"So show me."

They had to wait for her laptop to turn on for her to get to the files. Then she opened up the one file she'd been working on at home and then hit Save As so she could show him where it synced to. "See, it's here on the server where the rest of my work is."

She glanced up to see Dane staring around the small room.

"Anyone would know that though, right?"

"Yes."

"Then this is just temper and show dressing. They want you to know they are looking at you."

"And that means what? I didn't do anything."

Footsteps in the hallway had Dane sliding behind the doorway before he could be seen. Marielle stood in the middle of her small room hating the suspicion coursing through the space. She bent down and tried to collect the papers on her floor. The footsteps stopped. She froze. And peered around the corner of the desk. Candice stood there, her hands on her hips.

"There you are."

Marielle straightened up. "Yes. I'm back. What happened to my room while I was gone?"

Candice looked around the small room and shrugged. "It doesn't look like anything happened. Maybe the cleaning people knocked the papers over."

Marielle replaced the stack she'd picked up on the floor onto the desk. "Maybe, but not likely."

"Where have you been?" Candice asked, her voice sharper than usual, her gaze pointed. "You should have been here yesterday."

Marielle stared at her. "Why is that?"

"We had a companywide meeting."

"Really?" Marielle lifted her eyebrow in surprise. "I hadn't heard about it."

"Then you didn't read your email," she snapped. "And more than one was sent."

Marielle pulled out her chair. "I don't think I saw anything about it." She waited a half a beat. "What was it about?"

"Dr. Hudson was killed during a very unfortunate incident here earlier this week. It was the follow up and change in procedures we were going over at the meeting."

"Ah, I heard about his death on the news." Marielle managed to sound sincere and sad at the same time. It was hard with Dane behind the door and that added to the tension. She ran a hand over her head and pulled her chair back to sit down.

"There are going to be a lot more changes as well," Candice said. "And you will be one of them."

Uh oh. That didn't sound good. "In what way?" And why was she talking to her about it. Candice had nothing to do with her work.

"There will be no coming in on weekends to avoid us during the week," she started, already shocking Marielle with her nastiness. Then Candice just spewed as if a pustule of hatred had been festering for years. In truth Marielle had barely had anything to do with her.

Marielle cut off her nastiness. "First, I almost never come in on the weekends. I was gone on holiday last week, remember, booked off and approved as per company rules. I'm here now because I'm just home." She threw out her arm. "And what – were you in here destroying stuff?"

Candice gasped. "I would never do that. How can you say such things to me?"

Marielle heard the unhinged note in the older woman's voice. And the anger flaring. "I don't know, maybe it was the rant you just went on." She threw up her hands. "Sorry for accusing you but someone went through my stuff."

"Maybe Dr. Hudson was looking for something. You wouldn't mind him going through your desk, would you? After all, he was your personal friend."

Her stomach almost heaved at the thought. "No, he was your special friend."

The old woman's face paled quickly. Then flushed bright red in anger. "We'll see about your job too. You need to realize who is in charge here – and it isn't you."

"Why are people being laid off?" She was in a different position as a student, but she had no illusions about her future at the company. And if half of what they suspected turned out to be true, they weren't someone she wanted to work for long term anyway.

"Of course management shuffles all the way down. I've been here for decades. It always changes and yet never changes." She sniffed. "This time it might be different. They don't seem to have appreciated Dr. Hudson. They aren't doing something in his memory – nothing. It's like he walked out that door and never came back on his own accord."

"Did the police ever find out anything about his killer?"

Candice shook her head. "Not that I've heard."

Marielle watched as her eyes brightened with unshed tears. And felt immediately sorry. She'd been insensitive. Hadn't she pointed out to the guys his morning that Candice had been very close to Hudson – or appeared to want to be closer. Of course his death had been terrible, but for Candice it was horrible – as in life destroying.

"I'm so sorry about his death," she said gently. The other woman nodded and hurried away in the same direction she'd come from. As her footsteps finally disappeared, Dane came out from his hiding place.

He had an odd look on his face.

"What's the matter?" she asked him.

"Interesting personality."

"I said she's acerbic."

"You did. But she's also more unhinged at this point than I'd have expected." He stared out the direction she'd gone. "I couldn't see her clearly, but did she appear to have slept in her clothes at all?"

Surprised, Marielle cast her mind back. She'd been so scared that Candice would see Dane that she hadn't really noticed. But...maybe.

"She's always given the appearance of being slightly rumpled. At least lately, and she was a little more this time maybe. But why on earth would you think she'd slept in her clothes?"

"The way she spoke, her feelings for the doctor who'd been shot. Her erratic speech." He glanced around the room. "As if she hasn't been able to separate from him."

"But he's only been dead a few days. It's not as if she's had a chance to separate."

"Sure, but you're here on a Saturday for a specific reason. So is she. You know what your reason is, do you know what hers is? Or is it because she feels so close to him that she's here and can't leave. Because this is where her connection to him is. If she leaves the job then she separates more from him."

Marielle couldn't imagine. Then again she'd never loved anyone to that extent – except her mother. She slid a sideways look at Dane. He was special but he was also not for her. Too bad.

"Now what brought that look on your face?"

"Thinking about loving someone so much you can't leave the place you associated with them. That would be very odd."

"And maybe very beautiful," he said, surprising her. "Think of the depth of emotion that few people ever experience."

"I suppose. But it's also creepy. I wonder if he even liked her." She shook her head and clicked a few buttons to sync up her work. She had the USB attached that she used as a backup copy. The files were being transferred now.

"This shouldn't have anything to do with me, you know. All the work is here."

"But it's not finished, so maybe they want you to finish it for them as their guest."

"Then why try to kill me," she said practically. "That makes no sense."

"Clean up loose ends? And another possibility is that they weren't trying to kill you…"

She snorted, her gaze on the laptop as it worked away and the monitor as it transferred files. "Really? They hoped to incapacitate me with a bullet?"

"Or you weren't the target," he said calmly.

Slowly raising her glance, her mind shifted from work to the shooting and understood. She bolted to her feet and raced toward him. She reached out and grabbed his shirt, her eyes staring into his. "Oh my God. Were they trying to kill you this time?"

HE WASN'T SURE if he should have mentioned it or not but given her reaction, he was damn glad he had. He wrapped his arms around her and tugged her up tight. She shook his shirt impatiently. "Answer me, were they trying to kill you?"

"Maybe." What was he supposed to say? It wasn't like he knew the killer or understood what was going on in his mind.

"If they want to take you to do the research for them, then it's not an easy thing to do while you have a guard. Take out the guard and it's a simpler process."

"The same as grabbing my mother?"

He nodded. "And your mother has a guard around the clock."

"Who they might want to kill as well?"

"Right. It's hard to second guess who is doing what or when right now."

She glanced back at her work then out to the hallway. "I don't know what I can do. I can't destroy the information as it is kept on servers I can't access. They have backup files everywhere."

"Right. So maybe give it to the source that might be able to help."

She sent him a wry glance. "You mean the government."

He shrugged. "I know they have a bad rap in many ways but they aren't all bad, and they are trying to save lives. Our soldiers' lives."

"I'm not sure what I'm allowed to do," she said quietly. "I'll need to talk to my Ph.D. committee and see what their understanding is with Tenesco." She rubbed her temple.

"I can't see Tenesco liking any government interference." Then his voice changed as he added, "Unless it's a government contract as their money is good and the contracts lucrative."

She blinked. "I hadn't thought of that."

"But we'd have to make sure the company isn't behind the deaths or the espionage."

"Lord, I hope not. I've really enjoyed working here. Thought they were honorable. But there are always a few people who are much less so. But maybe the old owners were and after the takeover, not so much."

"Or the reverse. Nothing can be determined right now. In fact, I think we've been here long enough." He stopped and cocked his head. "Is there a back way out of the building?"

"Actually there is," she said in surprise. "I used to use it to avoid a coworker."

He stilled. "What coworker?"

"Dave. He had a thing for me and wouldn't take no for an answer."

"Why haven't we heard about Dave before?" He tried to tone down the harsh tone, but it was damn hard when he was only just now getting this information. Cell phone in hand, he was already texting his team. "What was Dave's last name, when did he work here, what was his relationship with the rest of the company?"

Startled, she gave a half laugh. "It was nothing, honest. I have no idea what his relationship was here, but he was gone months and months ago."

"Before the day is over, we'll know," he said. "Let's grab what you need and leave. We're late."

"Late for what," she asked in bewilderment. "Where are we going?"

"Out. We've been here too long." And instinct was screaming at him to run. Now. He peered into the hallway while she packed up her laptop.

"We need to go," he snapped, turning back to find out what was taking her so long.

She was back at her desk and clicking buttons. Then she pulled out drawers to collect her belongings. She grabbed up the pages she'd collected off the floor and stuffed them into her bag.

"Hurry."

"I'm almost done," she cried softly. "It needs another minute." She stared up at him, her eyes huge orbs. "What's wrong and why the panic now?"

"Instinct," he said in a clipped voice. "And we're going, *now*." He grabbed her arm and led her out the door still protesting. "Which way to the back exit?"

Finally, as if understanding the urgency driving him, she turned to the right, the opposite direction Candice had gone and said, "This way."

CHAPTER 21

H ER HEART POUNDING from his urgency, she almost ran down the hallway, her large bag with her laptop and papers under one arm and her purse slung over her other arm. This day was not turning out the way she'd expected it to. Not that she had much of an inkling of the day ahead except running away from bad guys was *not* it. Why would they be here? Again the stupid information was on the computer system. Any decent hacker would be able to get it.

She took the stairs and led Dane down to the maintenance level. With any chemical research there were huge HVAC systems and the maintenance room was a decent size. With a small back door. Thankfully the room was empty. She led him to the door and opened it, only to have him abruptly drag her back. She glared at him but he wasn't watching. He peered around the corner of the door to check that it was safe.

Because of that she ignored his high-handedness. It was hard to get upset when the man was protecting her.

"Okay, let's go."

He reached behind for her and together, holding hands they raced out. They had another corner to navigate before they reached the parking lot. He'd parked at the very back where it was hidden by large trees. Smart man.

No – experienced man in shitty situations. Did he ever turn off? Could he ever? Or did he live a life of constant danger? Of always being under attack. That had to be wearing. And hard mentally.

Not an easy way to live for any of them.

"Are you okay?" she asked him.

He turned and looked at her. Was that surprise lighting those so very magnetic eyes. "Of course. Why?"

How to explain? "It just seems like you're never relaxed. You're always on guard. Always looking for enemies out there."

"I am," he said gently. "There are people after you, remember."

She smiled. "And thank you for taking such good care of me." In a quick shift of mood, she reached up and kissed his cheek. "I mean that."

"How about you thank me again later," he said, his voice low and velvety soft. "And I'll show you how much I want to keep you alive."

She grinned. "You've got a deal." She laughed. "I guess that means I'll be alive for a little while longer then if you have any say in it."

He laughed. "Now if that were only so easy." He froze, his arm shooting out and shoving her behind him. She waited, crouched against the wall, her heart beating like an imprisoned butterfly.

Then suddenly, her hand was grabbed. He whispered, "Run, now." And together they raced straight ahead. She didn't dare look at what had bothered him, afraid that if she saw someone they'd see her too. There was a long line of trees at the parking lot. He pulled her to a stop in the middle of the greenbelt and studied the surroundings.

"Wait."

She gasped to catch her breath, her heart still slamming against her rib cage. All she wanted now was to be back in the safe house. This was not how she wanted to live.

At his motion, they walked quickly to the SUV. He unlocked it and walked to the driver's side. Casual and unconcerned. She tried to match it but it was damn hard. The sun was shining and the blue sky above made her wonder how such darkness could lie undetected in the world that seemed so nice otherwise.

Once inside, he started up the engine and pulled the big rig out of the parking lot. He made a strangled sound then made a sharp left and quickly picked up speed. She stared behind them, trying to see what bothered him.

"What was wrong back there?"

"One of the men we saw in Germany was speaking with another man out front."

She slowly digested that news. "The offices are closed."

"Right, but the one man appeared to be in a business suit so whether it was a private meeting or an accidental meeting I don't know, but…"

"I'm not a big believer in coincidences," she said. Twisting back around she studied his hard jaw. "I gather neither are you?"

"No, I'm not and I don't like to leave anything to chance."

Right. Of course not. She loved that he was so take charge, never leave anything to chance type of guy. It made her feel safe. Secure. "Where are we going?"

He glanced in the rearview mirror. "Not home, that's for sure."

She spun again and looked behind her. "Are we being followed?"

"That black car has been on our tail since we pulled out of the parking lot."

"I didn't see it there."

"It wasn't. It was parked out front."

"Oh," she said in a small voice. "I never noticed."

"Well, it saw us, whether it has identified you or me I can't say, but they are staying wonderfully close."

"As in making a mistake of staying too close?"

"No, they are used to this. As in pros."

Pros. Oh shit. Then another thought occurred to her. "Any chance they are on our side?"

He grinned. "Yes, actually, a good one. But I'm not going to get a chance to find out." He took a sudden turn to the left and pulled into a huge mall. He whipped into a covered parking roundabout and then up several levels before pulling into an empty spot and parked. Then he tugged her down so they couldn't be seen from the back.

"That's a little too simple, isn't it?"

"Maybe, but they are going to be whipping up here pretty damn fast too."

Sure enough, another vehicle came racing up behind them, tires squealing, and past them before they were seen.

Dane, a feral grin on his face, said, "Got him."

DANE REVERSED THE big SUV back down two turns to the exit on the far side. He whipped across, down and back out onto the street. It happened so fast, he wondered if she understood what he'd done. He was in the middle of the traffic and bearing right then left and out onto the highway where he needed to go. And still weaving until he figured he was safe again, only then did he slow.

"Are you done?" she asked in a shaky voice.

He glanced over at Marielle, surprised to see her gripping the door as if she was afraid she'd be launched out of the vehicle. "It wasn't that bad, was it?"

She shook her head. The motion too fast, too strong and a little too wild. Reaching across, he held out his hand, waiting for her to place her hand in it. She did slowly. He squeezed her hand gently then laced his fingers with hers. "I'm sorry."

"Don't be. At least now you know we were being followed."

"Hmmm." He checked out the rearview mirror followed by another look at the side mirror. No one was on their tail. "It looks like we're clear."

"Ya think?" She snorted and took a quick look out the back window. "I couldn't follow you, and I'm inside the vehicle, so I can't imagine anyone else being able to."

He laughed. "Dodging a tail is not exactly something we're taught to do, but over time we've gotten good at it." He glanced behind and laughed. "Besides, Hawk and Shadow, are still with us – what a piece of work he is."

"You're really close to the team, aren't you?" She smiled at him as she looked for Hawk behind them.

"Team, squad, brothers, we've been called a lot of names." He changed lanes, using only one hand, the other still holding hers. "They are my brothers in every way that counts. We've been together for a long time. I've never trusted anyone as much as I trust them. There are others in our group, but I love working with these guys."

"You all have an obvious bond."

"We've been through a lot together," he admitted. "But we're stronger for it."

"And I appreciate it. You've all done a lot for me. I'm grateful."

Hell, gratitude was the last thing he wanted from her. She fascinated him. He wanted her in a big way but so far outside of a chaste kiss, she'd shown no real interest. No, that wasn't true. She'd shown interest. He was the one holding back in that he didn't want her to be another one night stand. He wanted what his buddies had. Someone special. For life.

He hated to admit it but for the first time, he was jealous of his buddies. And hated to feel that way. They were all good men and deserved to have the woman of their dreams. That each had that special woman fall into his lap just added to his mixed feelings.

In his world, there were always women, waiting and willing on a nightly basis. Sometimes more than one at a time. He'd never lacked for sexual partners. In a way, sex had turned into a sport. It was only now he realized he was tired of the same game.

He didn't want it to *be* a game anymore. He didn't want to play at it anymore. Or even have sex, he wanted to make love. Have the person he was with be the best thing that had ever happened to him and wake up to her every day for the rest of his life. When he'd entered the military, just the thought of all the willing women had made his day. He'd taken full advantage of it. Way more than his share. They all had.

But it wasn't the same anymore.

He wanted more. So much more.

The question now was – who was Marielle to him? Besides someone he already cared about – what did she want? Did what she want have anything to do with *him* longer than a one night stand?

Lord, he hoped so.

CHAPTER 22

"YOU'VE GONE SO quiet," Marielle said, her fingers still linked in his. She loved the contact. "Did I say something wrong?"

He laughed. "Not at all." He squeezed her fingers then let go so he could turn on the radio. She settled back to listen to the country twang that filled the inside of the vehicle. He was a country music lover? Interesting. She wished he'd hold her hand again though. The world didn't seem as scary when she had him.

She shifted slightly closer, gaining comfort in his presence. He was a good man.

She was due something special in her life. But was he going to be the one to fit the job? She'd never been that lucky before. Her boyfriends had been average, not knockouts like Dane. Hell, the whole team were that same alpha male that women went nuts over. She'd always backed away from thinking that there'd be a way she could compete so now she didn't know what to do. She didn't want to compete – she wanted there to be no competition. Just him and her. And that was a dream of all dreams. And so not happening.

She gave a slight snicker at the thought.

He reached over and grabbed her hand. "Hey, what was that for?"

"It doesn't matter."

"It does to me," he said quietly. "Everything you do matters."

"Really?" She looked over at him hopefully then realized what he meant. "Of course it matters. It might pertain to our current nightmare."

"Not just that," he said. "I care."

But he wouldn't say anymore.

She was desperate to push but knew better. She backed off completely. The SUV moved at a steady pace and for the second time she realized she had no idea where she was in a city she knew well. She tried to read the road signs, but they were moving at such a fast clip it was hard to do. Instead of putting a crick in her neck she leaned back and closed her eyes.

She was still so damn tired. This mad panic then calm then panic, it was wearing her down.

"Have a nap. We're still fifteen to twenty minutes from the house."

"That far still?"

"Yes, when I was evading the tail I ended up going in the opposite direction for a bit. By the time we backtracked we're still out a good fifteen miles or so."

"Interesting. I couldn't place where we were and I'm still lost." She yawned. "And I'm still so damn tired."

"Sleep," he encouraged. "You don't need to do anything right now but rest. As we never know when we'll have to run again, you need to power nap to keep up your strength."

"Or we could just go home and have this all go away." She watched as a huge stand of popular trees flashed by. "Everything out there looks so normal. How can that be?"

"For ninety-nine percent of the world, it is normal. Just your normal isn't theirs. Right now your world has flipped. It will right itself but could take a little longer than you'd like."

"It already has."

She closed her eyes for several minutes and forced herself to think of pleasant things. Her eyes popped open. "Would someone remember to feed Masters?" Then she realized what she'd said and giggled. "Considering that no one has been texting you like mad over a psycho cat wanting food, I guess all is fine at home."

He laughed. "That tomcat is just fine. Besides, you'll see him in a few minutes." He turned the SUV to the left and then a quick right.

She recognized the street and the long line of pretty maple trees lining the block. "The trees here are beautiful."

"They are." He pulled the SUV into the driveway and turned off the engine.

"We're home."

"If that's what you call it." She hopped out, grabbed her bag and walked to the front door. And found the door ever so slightly open. She backed up one step then another. "Dane?"

"Get behind me," he snapped, pulling his gun out from behind his back.

A gun she just now noticed. He pushed the door open and took a half step inside, gun at the ready. She tucked in behind him. Surely with all the men here nothing could have gone wrong. Masters. Oh no. She'd left him behind. If anyone had seen him they'd know she was here.

Was Masters okay? She wanted to race inside and find him but knew she had to let Dane go first. She needed to take some self-defense courses if she survived.

And that was what she'd just wanted to explain to Dane. Under the curtain of normalcy this nightmare continued. Life was so normal looking. And at times normal feeling – but in reality her world was a long way from normal. It was a light veneer of normality that was fake. She'd get comfortable and think the danger was over then something else would happen and she'd be caught up in the same damn terror.

Panic, calm, panic. Her body was ready to stay in panic mode and that couldn't be a good thing.

"Psst."

Startled she looked over at Dane. He was motioning for her to come behind him. She took several steps, her heart in her throat. She didn't want to know what was inside, but could hardly stay outside. She took a deep breath and ran up to him. He reached out and grabbed her hand and tugged her up against him. He crept around the corner. She followed.

An odd noise sounded from deep inside the house. She swallowed. Had Hawk returned with them? Was he back up in the tree where he'd been earlier? She hoped so but where were the others? Always watching. Always on guard. Shadow and Hawk had taken those roles more often than not, but then who was here now?

Then she heard a sound that chilled her heart.

A loud meow. She went to race past Dane, but he grabbed her and tugged her backwards. "Stay here."

She glared at him, but he forced her behind him as he did a thorough sweep of the downstairs. No one and nothing. In the kitchen Masters was sitting on the counter, his tail flicking in irritation. "Oh, I think he's hungry."

She ran over and picked the cat up, giving him a huge hug. She ran her hands over him, checking he was okay. "He seems to be fine." She opened up a cupboard and pulled down a can of food. "I forgot to feed him before we left." She quickly opened the can and dumped it in a bowl. "He must be starving."

Masters' head disappeared into the bowl instantly. She laughed. "See. That's what he wanted all along."

She reached out and stoked Masters' back. "What a beautiful boy."

He couldn't be bothered lifting his head. She smirked. "That's okay, I understand. A cat is king."

She turned, looking for Dane, who she'd thought was still standing behind her. And found no one. Damn. Had he gone upstairs to check that the house was empty? It would make sense. His team was here somewhere?

As she turned back to Masters, she realized Dane was there, but with an angry look on his face.

He walked toward her. She ran toward him. "What's the matter?"

"Leave, right no–"

"She's not going anywhere, are you Marielle?" A dark face slid out from the shadows. One she recognized from her lab at Tenesco.

Marielle shook her head. "Dr. Hoerner? What are you doing here?" she stared at the one man she really enjoyed working with. How could this be? Was he involved? Was she such a lousy judge of character? How could this man be on the wrong side of the team?

"You shouldn't have come back to the labs if you hadn't wanted to see me again."

That made no sense. At the obvious confusion on her face he sneered, "I never could see why they kept an eye on you. Your mental process is so damn slow. It makes no sense that you made the discovery."

"I process differently," she said in a low voice, her mind already racing on the implications. "Besides I wasn't looking for this discovery. It just happened."

"And that's the really sad part," he snapped. "It's only after you stumbled in that discovery..." he twisted his face while his tone made the word sound like an insult to the hard working chemists around the world, "that the company asked me to keep a particular eye on you."

She wanted to shake her head again but figured he'd really get mad at her slowness. Yet what he was saying versus what she understood wasn't the same thing. "Why?"

He snorted and waved a snub nosed gun around. She glanced at Dane's face, but with the bored look and his crossed arms, he made it seem like this was just an irritation in the day. She'd trusted him so far so she decided to take her cue from him.

"That's what I mean. You just don't get it, do you? Nothing is secret and everyone wants to know when something interesting happens. Especially something this interesting. And there is always someone there ready to pay for the information."

"So Tenesco isn't part of this nightmare, or it is?" she cried, wanting something clear for once. "I love working there, thought they were honorable."

"Hell, they are. At least this branch but they have no idea what is happening at other branches and the other two offices have hooked up with a bigger badder company into some major shit." He smirked. "Spying is lucrative and having an innocent arm in the US has given the big company entrance to a whole new sea of research. Only now you're meddling in shit you aren't supposed to be."

"I'm not doing anything. I went for a holiday to Germany to spend time with a favorite professor and everything blew up."

"That's because you're so stupid. It wasn't a holiday. It was a grooming session. To see what the company could offer you to make you work for them willingly. Only Michaels wasn't so sure anything would work with you being so moral and upright. I see you stole his cat though, so maybe you're not so high and mighty after all."

He snickered gleefully as if having found her weak spot.

When the right fist smashed into his nose, and the left came up under his chin, Dr. Hoerner had no time to react. The gun flew through the air harmlessly, landed and skittered across the floor. Marielle raced to grab it, snatching it up. She turned to look at the men, but Dr. Hoerner was already down and Dane stood over him. Not even winded.

Swede and Mason raced in from opposite sides of the room, guns out, ready for action.

"We saw him enter the house," Mason said. "We were getting into position when you pulled in."

"Glad he didn't get you two. When the house was empty I was worried."

Mason snorted. "Not happening."

The men grinned.

Marielle stared as they joked and laughed at the thought of someone sneaking up on them and taking them out. It could happen.

Dane caught her look.

He held out his hand. She ran over to him and gave him the gun gingerly, hating to even be holding it. He switched the gun to his other hand and held out his hand again. This time she smiled and placed hers in it. He tugged her close. "Are you okay?"

"Now I am." She stared down at the unconscious man. "It never occurred to me he would be involved. He was always so interested in my work. So friendly."

He squeezed her hand again.

"Like he said, they were keeping an eye on me." She swallowed hard and gripped his hand. "That really sucks."

"Maybe and maybe it also releases Tenesco from being an active part in this. That they have employees who are potentially on the wrong side makes them a large corporation involved in research that is highly sought after." He nodded at the unconscious man. "He is not unusual. He's weak and looking for an easy payout. This time, you. Next time, who knows? These activities always start out small and then grow. Once a moral code is broken and the legalities blur then it's much easier to take the next step on the dark side. Murder might be one step away or it could take twenty steps to get there. But given the right reward, they get there eventually."

She shivered. "That is a very difficult way to view the world."

"I've seen it over and over again." He dropped her hand and crouched down to the man's side. He checked his wallet and made a check of his ID. There was nothing new. "Interesting. He appears to be who he says he is."

"And you were expecting…"

He quickly ran his hands over the prone man, searching the pockets. He rolled him over and carefully studied the man's face.

"No cosmetic changes. No body modifications. No major identifying marks."

"But why are you looking at that?"

"Because often in espionage there are disguises used. Men with indistinct features so they blend in more."

"Nice. Not." She shuddered. "What do we do with him?"

"He's going to be picked up soon and taken for questioning."

"You don't want to question him yourself?"

He smiled. "I'll leave that to someone else."

She stared at him in surprise. "Now that I don't understand."

"Shadow is a wizard at getting information out of suspects. And I'd hate to take a treat away from him."

She laughed. "So now that makes sense. You like Shadow."

"I really respect the man. He can talk to beasts of all kinds – including human ones."

"And if he can't talk to this one?"

Dane grinned, but it was a feral movement that made her realize the man would talk – one way or the other.

She stepped back, needing to distance herself. "I forgot how the underbelly of the world worked."

"It works. That's key."

A sound came from behind her. She spun around and found herself peering around Dane as he moved so quickly to stand in front of her.

Shadow and Hawk walked in, guns drawn. When they saw Dane, they relaxed. When they caught sight of the prone man their gazes hardened. "I see you had all the fun while we were gone."

"What took you so long?" Dane asked with a grin. "Mason and Swede watched him arrive and were just coming in after him when we got here."

"Cooper and Bradley are on their way. Jace has joined in on the fun."

"Good. We could use the help."

"Where were these men before?"

"They were tugging other strings."

She nodded. He'd mentioned he worked with other SEALs earlier. Besides, it was all the explanation she was likely to get and maybe that was enough. They were all working to bring this to an end. And that's what she was looking for. An end.

"I appreciate it." She really did. "How many of you are there?"

"We usually work in groups of four or eight." He gave her a lopsided grin. "It can change. Depends on the situation."

Her eyebrows shot up. "Glad you have more men to draw on."

"We have all the manpower we need, when we need it. However," he shot her a look. "We rarely need it."

At that, she had to laugh. "Of course you don't." Her grin widened. "You are SEALs."

DANE GRINNED AT her. "Very true."

Then he turned his attention to the man at his feet. "Shadow?"

His buddy nodded. Shadow reached down and grabbed the man's collar and dragged him to the kitchen and the chairs.

Dane watched as they tied him up. Catching sight of Marielle staring in horror, her face already imagining something worse than what would actually happen, he walked over to stand between the two of them. And tugged her up against his chest.

"Let's get you upstairs, it's nap time."

She turned her gaze toward the stairs, eager, energy in her step. By the time she hit the stairs she was almost running. He understood. She needed to get away. To get out.

He followed her up the stairs. At the bedroom, she bolted toward the window where she tugged the curtains back and looked out. She was trying so hard to stay in control. But he could see the tremor. He stepped behind her and wrapped his hands around her shoulders, tugging her back against his chest.

"It's going to be okay."

"Are they going to hurt him?"

"Not likely. He'll talk way before it comes to that."

She gripped his hand. "Are you sure? And does that change anything? Does it make it easier to know that?"

"Of course it does. Life isn't easy."

"And when it goes bad, it goes really bad." She sniffled.

Shit. He hated a woman's tears. They broke his heart every time. He turned her around and tucked her up close against his heart. "It will be okay."

With a shake of her head she said, "No it won't be. The things that have happened." She sniffled again. "Are still happening...they won't be erased from my memory. They are stuck there for life."

"As are all the good things in life." He smiled down at her, trying to reassure her. "Remember that. There are two sides to everything. And in this case there are many really good things in life to keep in your mind as well."

She studied his warm gaze and asked, "Like what?"

He smiled and leaned over to kiss her forehead. "Like us. Like this." He kissed her again on her chin. Then on her cheek. And again on her nose.

She closed her eyes. He kissed first one closed eye, then the other. She tilted her head up higher. He brushed his nose against hers in a slow loving movement. She gave a gentle happy sigh. He kissed the tip of her nose. Then reached up a gentle finger and nudged her chin higher. He kissed the tip of her chin. Then pulled back slowly.

She whimpered in protest. She tugged him closer and laid her head against his chest.

"Nice," she whispered.

"Very nice."

"Hmmm." She smiled and nestled closer. He wrapped his arms lower and cuddled her close.

"Being together like this is a gift," he whispered. "And I for one want to enjoy it. Life is too precious. It's too damn short."

"And it's ugly as hell."

He chuckled. "Remember that the good stuff is there too."

"Like you." She leaned back and tilted her head up to look at him. "You are a gift."

And she kissed him. A gentle loving kiss with the softest touch, like a brush of butterfly wings beating against his lips. He wanted to kiss her more but didn't want to scare her off. And besides, her gentleness was unexpected. Special. He couldn't count on one hand the number of times he could remember having experienced such a thing.

She reached up again and kissed his chin then his cheek. As if copying his actions.

And he was a willing victim.

She murmured gently, her hands reaching up to tug his face down toward her.

He backed up a couple of steps and sat down on the chair, tugging her into his lap. Into his arms. Into his heart. He needed this woman, her gentleness. Her positive outlook on life. Her presence gave him balance. Gave him a sense of wholeness. He didn't want to do anything to mar it.

He could hear the raised voices downstairs. Needing to block the reminder from her mind, he tugged her forward and kissed her again. Taking the slow simmering heat between them into a deeper, darker drugged heat that had them both wanting more.

CHAPTER 23

S HE PULLED BACK and looked down at him. "Do you want me?"

He raised his gaze to her. So warm, caring, and so full of promise she melted against him. "Never doubt that."

"Is what we have for real? Or is it only a heightened sense of intimacy due to the circumstances?"

"I don't need to analyze it. Do you?"

"I don't know." She searched his gaze. "I want this but need to know if it's a fantasy or is it something better. Deeper."

"Better. Deeper for sure. Is it for real?" He stroked a hand up her back and slipped his fingers into her scalp. She closed her eyes, loving the feeling.

In a slow slumberous move, he tugged her down toward him. "I would like to find out," he whispered, his breath warm against her mouth. "The question is, would you?"

She teased his lips with one kiss then a second. "I want to. But I don't do one night stands."

"There is nothing one night standish about this. I should know. I've only had those."

She reared back and stared at him. "Really?"

He nodded. "Way back in high school I had a couple of longer relationships but not since." He smiled. "Women are all over the place, easy." He turned his gaze away. "I'm gone a lot. My lifestyle is dangerous and when we were off and home again, we all lived a swinger lifestyle."

"And that's changed?" She had already surmised what his love life was like. How could it not be? He was gorgeous, single and available. Women would line up. Had lined up. Would still line up. But she couldn't do that. Tonight maybe, because she desperately wanted him, this. Right now. But in the long-term she needed so much more.

Could she accept this for what it was?

"It has changed. Several times in the last year we've had discussions about how this has gotten old. It happened before Mason, but I think he was feeling it the worst." He stopped and kissed her again. "And Mason got lucky. He found Tesla and life for him has never been the same. We all wanted her." He grinned, his smile crooked, yet she didn't see any sense of loss in his gaze. "But she only had eyes for Mason. In truth they are perfect together," he said warmly. "Although she loves all of us and we love her."

"You're all very lucky." To have a relationship like that, with these men, yeah Tesla was the lucky one.

"Mason especially. And then it was Hawk's turn and we all realized Mason's luck wasn't a one off. It was something we could all find. Since then, we've stopped..." That crooked smile popped out again. "Or slowed our singles lifestyle down somewhat."

"While you looked around for something better."

"While we looked, waited." He tugged her slowly back down and whispered, "And hoped."

She kissed him, his words reaching into her heart and finding a response she hadn't expected. She'd been waiting, looking and hoping too. Only she hadn't lived a life of danger or craziness where she'd needed to let off steam or reaffirm her belief in life after so much death. But she'd been waiting in her own corner of her world in her own way. Until now…

"And now?"

"Now I hope that means some of the lucky stardust came my way."

She kissed him first but he took over quickly, his tongue dueling with hers before sliding inside her mouth to caress her tongue and along her teeth. Picking her up, he carried her to the bed then walked to the door and closed it firmly. He returned to her side and sat down on the edge. She opened her arms. "Let's see if there is stardust for both of us."

He pulled her into his arms. "I would love to."

It wasn't quite what she wanted to hear but it was close. And a great place to start.

She smiled up at him and reached up for him.

The feel of his lips, the heat of touch, and now as if they both had the acceptance to explore this beautiful new step – to have this time, this moment to explore each other…it was special. Her heart rejoiced. She pulled back slightly, wanting to tell him something, but he wouldn't let her speak. He kept his lips on hers, his tongue sliding deep within. She forgot what she'd been going to say… His warm breath bathed her face, his lips not even a heartbeat away as he shifted her in his arms. She relaxed back into the warm bedding. He moved to lie beside her then tugged her so she sprawled half on top of his chest.

She was fine with that. She stared down at his beloved face. In truth, this was exactly where she wanted to be.

He urged her head down to him. And tasted, teased, a fire building between them that had her trembling in minutes and wanting so much more. He flipped over and tucked her under him. Yes. When he lowered his head this time, it was as if he was intent on proving she was his. As if branding her in all ways. He slid warm hands under her shirt to brush against her ribs and slid upward to cup swollen breasts. She cried out and arched into his hands. The shirt was tugged up and over her head, her arms tangled in the material. When she tried to tug her hands free, he held them above her head so she couldn't move. She watched him as he studied her. Her breasts plumped in the bra, swelling in need, her nipples hard and so damn ready.

But he waited. And waited. His gaze hot on her skin. Studying her belly, her breasts, her skin, the slope of her collarbone, the curve of her neck...then when she didn't think she could wait any longer, he bent his head. She whimpered as his lips brushed across her breasts then down to her ribs, rising up to kiss the spot between her breasts. Somehow, he released the catch on her bra.

She heard his breath catch in the back of his throat as the material fell away.

An unintelligible murmur escaped and he lowered his head, taking the nipple into his mouth and suckling deep. She moaned, twisting beneath him. He wouldn't let up, instead he slid over to give the other breast the same attention. She tried to release her arms so she could stroke him, touch him...but he wouldn't let her.

His free hand slid down across her belly to the clasp of her jeans. With a flick, he had it undone and several long fingers tucked inside her panties.

"Too many clothes," she whispered. "Take them off."

He released her arms to drag her jeans down her legs, throwing them to the floor in abandon. He stopped and stared. She glanced down to see her white lace panties the center of his attention. Her body melted a little bit more.

Leaning over, he kissed her hip bones, first one then the other, before sliding his tongue along the simple band. She shuddered. And pushed herself up so she could divest herself of the remnants of clothing still attached to her arms. Free at last, she reached for his shirt and dragged it over his head.

He gave a shout of laughter and hopped off the bed, stripping off the rest of his clothes, leaving them where they fell. When he returned to her, she slid the panties down and dropped them beside his clothes.

This time when he reached for her, he didn't just kiss her, he ravished her. His hands building the flames from the earlier embers until she twisted beneath him, her body humming in joy as her nerve endings woke to his touch. Hell, they woke up screaming.

Not content to lie there passively, she caressed his hard body, the long lines of his legs, his arms, the heavily muscled chest. God, she loved this.

She took a deep breath, filling her nostrils with his scent, the very essence of what made him who he was. A hunter. A protector. She reveled in the joy of being here with him. Loved everything about him. The instant response when she touched him, the sounds he made when she touched his erection. His willingness to let her do as she wanted. Priceless.

She cupped the enlarged spheres below, taking the weight in the palm of her hand. A shudder rippled through him.

In response, he reached down and slid two fingers into the damp curls waiting for him.

Her hips lifted, her heart pounding, her cries filling the room.

She tugged him toward her. "Dane," she whispered. "Come to me."

"Are you ready for me?" His fingers slid lower, stroking the outside of the plump folds. He found her wet, hot and waiting for him, and smiled. "Maybe you are." He reared up and settled between her thighs.

Holding her head with both hands, he kissed her as if there were no other women in his life. As if she were special. As if she were the "one."

She wanted that to be the truth so badly…

Just when she didn't think she could take anymore, he slid just inside her entrance…and waited.

She twisted sinuously up against him, whispering, "More, give me more."

Obligingly, he gave her more.

A little more.

"Enough," she cried and reached down to his hips and pulled him close. In a single thrust, he'd seated himself deep inside.

She groaned, and her legs instinctively widened, wrapping around his hips. When he still didn't move, she lifted up against him beseechingly.

"Don't do that," he growled, resting on his elbows above her.

"Don't do what?" she said, slowly retreating then thrusting up again. She had very little room to wiggle but it was enough as he groaned and started to move, setting a pace that was hard and fast and took her right to the edge.

And over it. She arched her back, crying out as the waves poured over her – and he drove again and again and rode her right through her climax.

A guttural groan ripped free of his throat as his own release poured through him. He surged into her one last time before collapsing on the bed beside her.

SHE FELL ASLEEP in his arms. He should feel guilty for being here. He was on duty, but he couldn't remember ever having wanted anyone like he wanted her. Not the sexual drive of a frantic couple followed by a righting of the clothing and walking away. Nor the heavy emotionless atmosphere, taking what was offered only to wake up alone, not remembering the woman he'd been with. This was…he didn't know. For the first time he had no words. He reached up and stroked a lock of hair back off her face, still shiny from the sweat of her release.

A release he'd given her. Now boneless, she slept like an infant. And he should be going downstairs to talk to the others. Hear what they'd learned and send the asshole off. He knew the man would be picked up today and taken to the base. What they did after that was none of his business. They could deep six him and he'd cheer. The man had pulled a gun on Marielle. So not allowed.

He shifted slightly away, a tender smile coming to his lips as she murmured and tried to nestle closer. He kissed her and kissed her and kissed her again. He couldn't stop kissing her. Light air kisses so as to not wake her but so hard to resist. He dropped his forehead to rest on hers. With supreme control, he pulled himself back and rose from the bed. He used the washroom, wanted a shower but knew there was no time so had a quick wash instead and quickly redressed. He stepped out on the deck and surveyed the darkness. Somewhere along the line it had become night. He watched Swede walk the perimeter of the yard. They were on watches. He checked his time and realized he'd be up next – if the schedule was still the same. With a last look, he turned and left Marielle alone to sleep.

In the kitchen he found Shadow on the computer and Mason busy mapping something on the table. He walked over and poured a coffee. They'd need food again. That was something he could do. He opened the fridge and realized someone had shopped. Swede was outside and likely Hawk too. He figured Cooper and Jace had taken the prisoner back.

He pulled out several large packs of steaks from the fridge and busied himself trimming and adding a spicy rub. With all the vegetables stacked up in the fridge, he prepped a large Caesar salad and steamed veggies. Then found potatoes and grinned. He was famished and starches were good for energy.

Happy to be doing something normal and feeling pretty damn fine, he ignored the looks from the men and cooked up a full dinner. Before putting on the steaks, he turned and asked the others, "Who is here?"

Mason said, "Cooper and Bradley took Dr. Hoerner. Jace went with them."

"Good," Shadow said from behind his laptop. "More for us."

"Did you guys learn anything?"

"Nothing new. He was paid by Michaels. Recruited by him. Everything seemed to run via him. He was in the know to some extent but not enough to have anything new."

"Yet with him now out of the picture, we still don't know

who is the problem."

"Does it matter? Take her home and we can go to Germany and take them down. We will have better intel over there."

Dane set the finished meal on the table as the others scurried to move their research materials out of the way.

"The problem is we don't have enough information. We have little league people, not the bosses. We keep taking out the small men but no one even knows who's above their immediate boss and with that level removed, no one knows who's above him." Swede took a bite of dinner and said when he could, "Smart really."

"So how do we find them?"

"We could shake down each of the others. One at a time. One will crack," Shadow suggested as he cut a slice of rare steak. "However, I'm tracking the money. Started with Michaels. He received quarterly payments, six figures. Regular for the last few years."

"Confirms what we knew."

"And the money came out of Germany."

"Any way to track other people's money?"

"Not legally," he said calmly. "However, the head of the Tenesco chemistry labs did not have the same type of payout. In fact, I can't find anything out of the ordinary."

"Too clean?"

Shadow cocked his head. Then shook it. "No. I think he *was* clean."

"What about her? Candice. Did you check her out?"

"I did. And there were regular small payments going back years."

Everyone at the table stopped and stared at him. "Small

amounts?"

He nodded. "They weren't much, but they added up to six figures over the years."

"So not blood money?"

"Hard to say. Maybe loyalty rewards."

Swede snorted. "Why so little?"

"Maybe it had been set in place so long ago that it was the right amount for the time. And the arrangement was agreeable for all parties so why change."

"Possible. Were the payments from Germany as well?"

"Yes." Shadow nodded. "I think she was keeping an eye on the place."

"A snitch," Dane said. "That would make sense."

"Any others at the company?"

"Not that I've found so far. However, if there were two there is a good chance of more."

"Three if you count Michaels, if you can research several years back to when he worked there," Marielle said from the doorway, her voice hesitant. "Is there enough dinner for me?"

"Of course!" Dane hopped up to grab her a plate. "I was hoping you'd sleep through the night."

"My stomach woke me, I think," she said with a smile as she took a seat at the table.

Dane cut her a slab of steak from a huge one and added a large portion of vegetables. He placed it in front of her and nudged the remains of the big Cesar salad. "I'm sorry you're not sleeping, but if your body needs food, you woke up at the right time." He found her a knife and a fork. "Dig in."

He retook his seat, his gaze lingering on her features. She looked rested. Good. He turned back to his plate and caught the look on Swede's face. That, *hey you did good* look. He narrowed his gaze back at him.

Swede gave him an innocent look in response, too innocent. His eyes twinkled with mischief. Dane shot him a look intended on setting him back in place, but as Swede's grin slid sideways, he knew he'd failed. As long as he kept his comments to himself.

Shit.

He ignored the others and tucked into his food. He appreciated a good meal and this one was good. When he was done, he stood up and cleared off his plate. He set up coffee next. It was empty again. He didn't know about the others, but he'd enjoy a cup. He stood at the window and stared out into the darkness. He'd head out and relieve Hawk. There was still steak and vegetables for him.

"Shift change." He grabbed his travel mug and filled it with coffee. He turned before he walked out and called back to Marielle, "Hawk will be in soon. Everyone is changing shifts, eating as they can before moving to the next shift." He narrowed his gaze at her. "Stay inside and away from the windows."

She turned to look at him. "I will be careful. The guys will look after me."

"Good." He walked to the door again and pushed it open. Hawk walked in as Dane walked to the door.

"There you are. All is well out there."

Dane nodded. "I never expected it to be any other way."

He tried to walk out but couldn't force himself to do so. Damn. He turned around, set his mug of coffee down and strode over to the table where Marielle sat staring up at him.

"Go back to bed and rest," he ordered.

When she opened her mouth to protest, he half lifted her up

from her seat and tugged her into his arms and kissed her. Long, hard and so damn thoroughly he knew it looked like he'd placed a stamp on her. And maybe he had. She was his and the others had damn well better know it.

He released her to slump back into her chair, then with a satisfied grin on his face, he stormed out into the night.

CHAPTER 24

SITTING BACK DOWN, her face hot and bothered, she couldn't stop sighing happily. She was a damn fool. And the men...they were busy trying to keep their gazes on the food in front of them. Mason was back looking at the map.

"What are you looking for on the map?" she asked him.

"Another safe place."

"For us?" She forked up a bite of food and chewed slowly as she considered it. "We can't stay here?" Too bad. She had lovely memories of the place that overrode the earlier horror. Almost...

"No."

Her stomach, initially overjoyed at the promise of food, started to rebel. "Right. When do we stop running?"

"When we have a target to go after."

"And Tenesco isn't it?"

"It is partly, but it could be that the American branch has no idea what the German branch is doing. It appears the three arms of the company were run originally by three brothers. Each in a different country."

She looked outside and watched Shadow approach. He came in, served a plate and set dishes to soak as he came over and sat down. He didn't look tired. None of them did. Unlike herself. And she'd slept. She glanced at her watch and realized she'd only had a nap. They had only gotten home a couple of hours ago. So much had happened since. "When are we leaving?"

Hawk checked his watch. "Sixty minutes."

"Oh." She quickly finished her plate, the lovely relaxed feeling she'd woken up with long gone. "I'll go pack." She washed her plate and escaped to her room.

It took less than five minutes to pack up her personal belongings and another five to locate her bag of stuff she'd removed from the lab. Masters took longer. By the time she had her coat and bags and pet, the men were already loading up the SUVs. Of Dane there was no sign. She tried to act natural as she got into the vehicle Hawk motioned at her to get into, but it was hard to not look around and wonder where he was hiding.

In the back passenger seat she slunk down and waited. Before she realized it, they were moving silently through the night. Only she couldn't see Dane.

The SUV turned onto the side street and toward the main road. She twisted to look behind them to see the second vehicle was a half block behind her. Her SUV, driven by Swede with Shadow riding shotgun, pulled off to the side. She opened her mouth to ask then closed it. Suddenly the door opened. She gasped then smiled as Dane slid into the back seat beside her.

He'd waited to make sure no one followed them and had crossed through the backyards and met them on the other side of the block. Smart.

He grinned, reached across and kissed her.

The SUV pulled back onto the main road and drove off into the night.

She lost track of the miles and direction they travelled. They were taking her somewhere safe and that was all she cared about.

Besides – she was with Dane. It was all good. By the time they came to a stop at another location, unloaded only what they needed and got her into a room in yet another house, she wondered if they were in the real estate business. Nice if they were but she doubted it. She wanted to ask a million questions but knew they wouldn't answer and at this point, she was too damn tired. When she saw the bed, she let Masters out, set up his food and litter box then took off her coat and lay down fully dressed. A blanket was thrown over her and then the bed sagged as someone lay down behind her. She smiled.

"Good night," she whispered.

His arm came around her, tugging her up close, and with his warm breath against her cheek, he whispered, "Good night."

SHE DRIFTED OFF to sleep so easily. Good. That meant she felt safe and trusted him and the others. He could power nap, particularly when under pressure, but this running away stuck in his craw. He needed to keep her safe, but never ending problems of keeping on the move impacted his ability to shut down. His mind circled with options but didn't find a solution.

When he knew she was deep asleep, he slipped off the bed and moved to the living room. Shadow was still pounding on the keyboard.

"Anything?"

He shook his head. "Everyone else in Tenesco looks clean."

"And the other branches?"

"I'm working on it but there are hundreds of employees."

"They'd have to be connected to Michaels. He's key in all of this."

Shadow stopped and looked up at him. "Suggestions?"

"His damn house and the hidden doors and rooms."

Shadow's gaze narrowed. "And the computer I didn't have much time to work on."

He glanced at his watch. "Do we know what happened to the house? Did anyone claim ownership? It's deeded to Michaels, but beyond that?"

"Not yet. Inheritance laws in Germany are not easy or fast or simple."

"Then let's go back."

Mason entered in time to hear that last bit. "Where?"

Dane explained.

Mason fired question after question. He looked at his watch. "We're not that far away in terms of flight time."

"Exactly." Dane glanced toward the bedroom where Marielle slept. "We could slip away now."

He hated to leave her. Really hated it. And knew she'd have the same reaction to waking up alone. But she was safe here. "I think we should leave her behind. Just two of us go." He hated to but all she did was nap. She needed more rest to fully heal. Not head off on another jaunt to Germany.

"Not happening," Marielle's voice came from behind him. She stood fully dressed and ready to go. As always. "It's a waste of a night's sleep if we're leaving now, but money doesn't seem to drive any of this operation, and besides, the sooner it's over the better. I agree we need to go back. There has to be something else there that will put an end to this."

Silence.

She could jeopardize everything, however…leaving her behind was going to be difficult. They had the manpower, but she also knew Michaels, the work in question, and might be a bigger help at the house. She was the one who had let them into the office.

"You need me," she said baldly. "I'm the one in danger here and I'm the one who knows the house."

"You only know the house slightly. We're all trained to detect if anything is wrong, and we're likely to find all the same places you might," Dane snapped. "You stay here. You're safe here."

She glared at him. "Sure, as long as you guys are here."

His voice softened when he realized she was scared to be alone. "Only a few of us would go." He glanced over at Swede. "Maybe Swede and I."

"And if you run into trouble?" she asked coolly. "You're a team. At least four of you should go. Then if you run into trouble you have each other."

He frowned. "We don't have four to stay with you then."

"Exactly," she said smoothly. "So I'd better come with you and then we'll all be safe."

He glared at her and the others chuckled.

"It's really not an option," she said. "Splitting up is a bad idea."

"We split up all the time," Dane said. "And keeping you safe is a priority."

"Well, then take me with you." And she gave a Cheshire cat smile. "How could any place be safer than with you?"

CHAPTER 25

I T WORKED. SHE held that smug satisfaction inside. He'd not appreciate her attitude, but in truth she was grateful for being with him. She did feel safe with him and his men. They'd proven over and over again that they cared. She'd hate to be with strangers right now, and as much as she wanted to be home with her mother, if that couldn't happen then here with Dane was her best option.

And it was more than that. The moments, even dangerous wrought filled moments with Dane, were precious. She didn't want to lose him and once this was over, she would. She wanted all the time with him she could have.

Now, in the back of the plane, wondering at the simplicity of air travel with the military, she watched and waited. They'd be there in half an hour. They were already descending. She stared around the no frills machine. She could get used to the simplicity.

And once again she had Masters with her, there was no one else to take care of him. It helped that she couldn't bear to part with him. They were a package deal. She *had* to say good-bye to Dane. She refused to say good-bye to Masters too. Not if she didn't have to.

Her fingers brushed against his silky fur. He seemed to be

fine with the new travel arrangements, curled up content in his cage once again.

"We're landing in ten," Dane said, sitting down beside her. He buckled up, checked that hers was still tight and dropped a kiss on her nose.

See, that's what was so special. He didn't give a damn if they were seen or by whom. He was comfortable in his skin. And in their relationship. Whatever that was.

Personally she only knew what she wanted it to be. And it wasn't there yet. Wouldn't likely get there either. She'd focus on the time she had.

"Good. Flying is much faster with you guys than flying commercial, isn't it?"

He nodded. "Flying commercial is a good reminder of the perks we have. Except this is work. So we need to get where we need to be *fast*."

It was faster than she'd ever seen. They landed, cleared customs, and were in a dark vehicle that resembled the US counterpart but with a few extra perks. Now it was still morning, and they were planning on driving right up to Michaels' house and go in. She'd deliberately not asked about the legalities of such a move but understood that someone was finessing that official approval in the background.

The sky was bright, the birds singing – yet the village appeared to be empty. She checked Dane's watch. It was still early. The farmers would be out milking the cows or feeding the livestock, but the rest of the villagers were likely snoozing in their beds. It wasn't even seven in the morning yet.

At the house, no one appeared to be home. Marielle picked up Masters and carried him inside. His bright eyes showed his interest, but he didn't cry out or show fear in any way. He knew the house better than anyone. They'd do well to let him out and roam on his own free will.

Maybe he'd show them where to go.

Inside the front door Marielle stopped, reminded by all that had happened since she'd been here just a few days ago. And the string of deaths that had happened since.

"Now, suggestions?" Dane asked.

Marielle turned in surprise to see the others looking at her.

"The hidden office first. And then I want to check for a lab."

Mason's eyebrows shot up.

Swede nodded. "I'm heading to the computer system. Keep me posted."

"I'm with Marielle," Dane said. "Either Mason or Hawk should come with us, and we need one to stand watch."

Minutes later they were sorted and heading in the various directions. Marielle smiled at the well-oiled machine of teamwork. At Dane's head nod, she led the way to the kitchen. She placed Masters' cage on the table and opened it. The big ole tomcat strode out as if unaware of his transatlantic trip and return journey to his home. He wandered the table then sat on his bottom, flicked a leg toward the ceiling and started cleaning himself.

She grinned. He was such a typical cat. Reassured that he was fine after all the travelling, she turned her attention to the many doors leading off the large commercial looking room. She watched Mason and Dane search the place while she racked her brain looking for bits of memories that might have something to do with this house. And came up blank. She'd hate for them to think she'd come on false pretenses and had nothing to offer. She studied the layout, then looked back at the hallway and considered the secret wall in the office – hiding a private room. Made sense. If she had a lab here, she'd want it private too.

Studying the wall again, she figured that if she wanted to get downstairs and have no one know, she'd need to have a set of stairs that no one could find. And the best place for that would be where the stairs were already. Use the same infrastructure but cut the staircase in half. So the second set of stairs could stay hidden and no one would know. She wandered back to the hallway and studied the imposing space. A huge winding staircase going up on the left to the second floor caught her attention. She knew the men had searched upstairs earlier, but it made no sense to have a lab up there. She dismissed the idea. No, if there was a lab here it would be downstairs. And given the age of the building it could easily have several downstairs.

She knocked on the wood of the walls close to the stairs to the empty lower level. She made a pass to the front door then came back on the opposite side. She wasn't sure what she was looking for but knew she'd recognize it when she found it.

Almost back to the kitchen entrance, she realized she was being watched.

She turned to see. Of course, Dane. He leaned against the door jamb, his arms crossed, watching her.

She frowned at him. "Aren't you supposed to be looking too?"

He laughed. "Oh I am."

Her frown deepened as she realized what he meant. Then rolled her eyes. Her next knock on the door sounded loud and clear and hollow. She grinned. Dane reached her side in seconds. "What did you find?"

"Not sure yet," she muttered. "But it's definitely not the same as all the other walls in here."

Mason joined them and it took another ten minutes to find the lever that slid a section of paneling back to show stairs hidden behind them. Instantly both Mason and Dane drew guns. She stared into the darkness, fascinated at the idea of a house of secrets. The men were more bothered about safety than she was.

Dane contacted the others and told them what had been found. When he was done he led the way forward. She followed with Mason bringing up the rear position.

Safe as they could possibly make her, she was delighted with her discovery and excitement bubbled through her veins. She could only hope there was a wonderful lab down here. And knowing Michaels, it was very possible.

They descended the stairs.

TAKING THE LEAD, Dane slipped down the stairs, ears trained on his surroundings. It was quiet. As they descended into the lower levels of the old stone mansion, he couldn't imagine what these stairs had seen in their lifetime. War torn surroundings decades ago and likely in its prime it had been at the heart of a different revolution. He loved to think of the history of a place like this. The people who'd lived and laughed and eventually died here. And those who took refuge in war times, so much less pleasant to remember.

The stairs took a corner to the left, he peered around, realized it was empty and continued his descent into the basement levels. How much effort and time would have gone into building this? Considering the walls were of stone, and possibly hand cut from the hillside, the process would have been even more labor intensive. There were no lights, and the deeper they went the darker it got.

He stopped on the last stair, turned to make sure the others were following, and stepped down on the cold stone floor. A hallway ran directly ahead of him with doors on either side dotting the passage. All were closed. He reached out a hand searching for a light switch. And found it.

Light flooded the area, giving it an eerie look.

But he was relieved the basement had been upgraded with electricity. With the others behind him, he walked to the first door and opened it.

He flicked the light on to see what appeared to be a small storeroom of some kind. He turned his attention to the door Mason was opening on the other side.

Marielle gasped with delight and stepped in.

Mason followed her with Dane hot on their heels.

"It's a lab," she cried. "Oh what a lovely set up."

Dane looked at her sideways. There were long tables on one side, an obvious chemistry set up on the end of one, but there were no windows or natural lighting. He glanced up at the drop ceiling to see a solid modern looking venting system. "He put money into this place," he said.

"He did," she agreed. "But his father was also a chemist, so maybe this has been a working lab for a long time."

Dane couldn't imagine. "Anything useful here?"

"Not at first glance, but there will be somewhere," she said. "There isn't anything new or different or science breaking here. Not that I'd expect to see the type of work he's doing at first glance, but as labs go, the equipment is pretty basic," she added, absentmindedly looking at a bookcase on the far side. "His notes and observations don't appear to be here." She opened a few drawers, shuffled through the papers stuffed inside.

"Then let's check the other rooms."

They filed out single file and checked the next room. A bathroom with a large modern shower.

"This is good to see," she said. "He's put in many safety features." She turned and opened the cupboards beside the huge shower and nodded. "This is more of a medical center than a bathroom."

At the next door they found a similar room to the lab but with less signs of occupancy, the tables clean but slightly dusty as if it hadn't been used for years. Still Marielle wandered through the room looking for something.

She shrugged and left, following Dane to the next room.

"This is the one we want," she cried as she dashed into the large office with several desks crammed full of paperwork and leather bound books. "These should be his lab books."

"Meaning?"

"They will be the ones that he used for his experiments. We all keep them." She picked up the first one and opened to the first page. "This one is from a year ago." She picked up the next couple and nodded. "They are all sequential and appear to cover the last eighteen months or so." She stacked them up on the desk, then turned to look around.

Dane watched her. She appeared to be more interested in the setup than in the research. And yet there was likely something she could learn from it. "You aren't reading his research?" he asked curiously.

She flushed. "No. It's not my style. Research is highly prized, secretive and I work on an honor system. If he was here to talk to me about it, great. But he isn't."

"And yet he discussed it with you before?"

A smile lit her features. "We discussed it for hours." She motioned to the books. "Technically all this belongs to his heirs, or depending on the contract, the company he worked for."

Mason stepped in. "That will be determined eventually, but if no one knows what's down here, it won't matter if they can't find it."

She nodded. "True enough but he was a brilliant chemist. His work should not be lost."

"And if it was chemical warfare for those fighting against your people?" Mason asked, his voice hard but steady.

She winced. "There's no easy answer is there?"

CHAPTER 26

S HE HADN'T THOUGHT to find herself in such a position. Professional and moral ethics butted up against each other for the first time. It was uncomfortable. To save lives though...that was priceless.

"We need to track down his heir," Mason said, pulling out his phone. "We can find that out soon enough."

With him chasing that down, Marielle walked the rest of the room fascinated at this personal insight into her old friend. And they *had* been friends. She might not have known who or what he was on the inside as well as she thought she had, but back when he worked for the same university, they'd been friends.

Somehow between then and now, things had changed for him.

She couldn't help but stare at his lifetime of work and hate to see it lost.

Dane came up and placed an arm around her shoulder. "You okay?"

She nodded, hating that moisture was collecting at the corner or her eyes. "It's just hitting me now. He's really gone."

Spinning in a circle, she realized how much he'd left behind. Undone. In progress. "He was brilliant you know."

"And yet he wanted you to join him? Are you just as brilliant?" Dane asked, a dry tone to his voice.

Her laughter pealed across the room, bringing a smile to his face. "I wish."

"You must have been special to him in some way," Mason said in an odd tone. She turned to see him staring down at his phone.

"Why's that? Because he wanted me to come work for his company?" she scoffed. "Not likely. He just wanted the information I tripped into."

"If that was all, why are you listed as a beneficiary in his will?"

"What?"

She stared at Mason, hating that she might come under a cloud of suspicion because of this. If she was listed, then she'd have motive for killing him. "I don't understand."

"Nothing to understand." Dane turned back from the cupboards he was studying. "He wanted to leave you something." He turned further around to face Mason. "Does it say what she was given?"

"Only partly and that's because of the item," Mason said dryly. "She inherited Masters."

"Oh that's great," she cried with a huge smile. "And makes a lot of sense. I always looked after that big baby. I told him many times that if he couldn't look after him to let me have him."

"And apparently he listened." Mason shrugged. "Interesting."

"And normal," she said firmly. "More people have to make allowances for their pets in the event of an unexpected death. Hell everyone should regardless. Death is not particular. He goes after everyone."

Mason laughed. "True enough."

"Anything else of interest in the will?"

"The lawyers are going through it now, so not sure. That note listed as an amendment to be opened upon his death."

"So Masters wouldn't suffer." Marielle nodded, liking her old professor a little more after finding out so much that was negative. At least he'd taken care of those in need. "Hopefully the lawyers can get to the bottom of this, so the new owner can come and deal with all this research."

"And just what would the new owner do?" Mason asked curiously. "Especially if they don't know him. Such as a distant relative."

"That would be a shame. I imagine they'd come through here and throw everything." She frowned, hating the idea. "If the beneficiary was a colleague, I'd hope they'd go through and preserve his work." But how. She'd never come up against the problem. Thankfully she wasn't the one having to deal with the problem now either.

They walked back out to the hallway and continued to open the other two doors. In one was a small bed and dresser. They all stared at the sleeping room in silence.

"Why?" Dane asked.

She shrugged. "I imagine to stay close to his work when he was deeply involved in his research. Alternatively for a colleague."

"And not as a guest in the upstairs bedrooms?" Mason said. "I don't like the look of this room at all."

Marielle walked toward the bed and lifted the single pillow then dropped to her knees to look underneath. It was clean and empty. The clean part bothered her as much as anything. "It's recently been swept out. As if expecting someone."

Inside her stomach rumbled. She hated the next thought. "Please tell me I wasn't to be his next guest in this room."

"I can't say that yet." Dane opened the small closet to find it empty. He turned in a slow circle as if trying to understand the extent of the room's purpose. Then he stopped and stared.

Marielle followed his gaze to the door. And the thick lock on the door. A lock that locked from the outside.

"So this wasn't a guest room but rather a cell?"

Dane nodded. He opened the door and walked outside to study the lock system. "Definitely to keep a prisoner."

She walked out beside him, Mason was still studying the small empty room then exited as well. "Not a comfortable existence."

"No bathroom," she said. "So couldn't have been for long term."

"Maybe." Dane's voice was calm, quiet. He opened the far room to see yet another small cell like bedroom. She followed him inside and realized this one had a bathroom. "Okay this is freaking me out."

"And so it should." Mason pointed to the bedroom and the covers and the small envelope sitting on the top.

An envelope with her name on it.

DANE REACHED THE bed in two strides. "What the hell is this?"

"A message apparently." She lifted the envelope and carefully opened it. The letter was unsealed. Inside was a folded single sheet of paper.

She read the message out loud.

"*Dear Marielle, I'm delighted to finally have you with me. I was hoping you'd come willingly. But rest assured, it was planned for you to be here anyway. There was a time when I thought you'd see things my way. Or at least open you to the delights of money and power. The thrill of the covert. The power of belonging to something bigger.*

"*Now I realize you will never be swayed to my way of thinking. Honestly I'm not a fanatical believer of anything but the power of the buck. I'm just a money hungry type of guy.*" She could almost hear his snigger. "*And be assured that what I am doing is bringing in very good money. But I need you to make the really big score. I know what you have discovered and the value that you haven't.*

"*You're so naïve that you don't realize the potential gold mine in your hand. Well, I do. And I need your research so that I can make the big score and stop with the little drips and drabs. I have no idea how long I have left to live, but I do know that I don't want it to be living like I have been. I'm meant for bigger and better things. You could win a Nobel peace prize – or you could earn a hundred million dollars. At one time I'd have loved the first. Now I realize that it's only the second one that has any value.*"

"*And that you have the means to give that to me – and so far haven't – is unacceptable.*" She paused and swallowed hard before continuing.

"*You'll remain here as my guest until you see things my way.*" She rubbed her temple, her mind struggling.

"*PS. You might not see me for a while. But rest assured your keepers will take good care of you.*"

Her voice fell silent as she lifted her horrified gaze to the men's grim faces. "He was going to kidnap me and keep me prisoner?"

Dane hated to see the shock in her face. The betrayal of a friend. But the sheer fury in her voice restored his faith in her. She could deal with this.

And he could help. "Remember, he didn't succeed. You escaped. We've kept you safe. You're not going to be locked up in this hell hole."

She flashed him a hard smile. "Glad to hear that." She cast a final look around the cell, hating the proof of her intended future. She hated this and said, "Can we leave now?"

"Definitely. Come on." He stepped aside so she could leave. Out in the hallway, Dane, Mason at his side, checked out the remainder of the rooms. Making sure there were no exits or secret rooms. "Looks like that's it," Dane commented as he ran his fingers over the old stone wall at the end of the hallway. "No other doors coming in or out."

"Good. It's an interesting layout, but not a place I'd like to spend much time in."

"It doesn't make sense," Marielle said. "He got out of the house while you were here. He didn't walk out the front door, he snuck out somehow without you seeing him."

"So you're thinking there's yet another exit." Mason turned around in a slow careful movement. "If so, it's not here."

"It might not be," she said. "But I definitely got the impression from him that he had a secret way in and out."

Dane led the way back to the lab. He'd already gone through some of the paperwork. He'd hoped for a ledger, a little black book of some kind detailing his plans. It would likely be computerized, hopefully Swede or Shadow would have found it. The cell and letter went a long way to convicting the dead man though.

Back upstairs, the three stood in the main hallway for a moment, watching the hidden door close quietly and effectively disappearing into the hallway. Marielle turned to the office where Swede and Shadow were working on the electronics. She called back to the others, "Any idea if there's a way to get a plan of the house? Blueprints showing all the secrets?"

"If there is, the guys will find it," Dane said beside her. "Shadow's a wizard but Swede is almost as good."

CHAPTER 27

MARIELLE TOOK UP the comfiest looking chair in the office and still winced. It might have appealed to the Victorian era crowd, but she'd take comfort over antique any day. And given the size of the house and the sheer amount of antiques in the house, someone was going to have a lot to deal with here.

"Okay, found the city planning department. There's been no building permit issued in the last twenty years and the records are not online before that. Likely only in microfiche at this time. So that will require someone to go down and request the films to skim through if we think it's of any value."

"And that's presuming there is anything to find."

"You'd think he'd have something here that would give him the details of the house. Passed down from generation to generation."

"There probably is." Mason walked over to the bookshelves lined from floor to ceiling. "But where? They could be any-where."

She stood up and stretched. "I need to find a bathroom."

Mason nodded to the hallway. "First door on your right."

"Nice. I'll grab Masters and bring him back here at the same time." She headed to the hallway and the bathroom. When she was done, she washed her hands, sprinkled a bit of cool water on her face and returned to the men. Just as she was about to reenter the office, she caught sight of Masters dashing down a hallway. A hallway she didn't remember. "Masters? Come here, sweetie," she called out. "Stay close please."

The place was huge. She couldn't imagine all the hidey holes he'd be able to hide in. She ran after him.

"Masters? Masters. Masters!" she called out. But of course he wasn't going to answer her or respond. First off he was a cat, and that meant he'd do things when he felt like it and never because she requested it. She laughed as she caught sight of him up ahead. Sitting and waiting for her as if to say, "What took you so long?"

She reached him finally and bent down to scoop him up. As she walked the small area he'd brought her too, she realized it looped back around to the kitchen. Nice. She looked down at him and asked, "Did you eat your dinner?"

In the kitchen she checked out his food dish and smiled. It was licked clean. She washed the dish and refilled it. Masters kept up a high pitched conversation as she worked. There wasn't much else to offer in food from the cupboards. She could come up with a pasta meal in a pinch, but it felt wrong to help herself. The fridge was empty of all fresh fruit and veggies. As if the professor either hadn't lived here or had been away and was only recently home. She wondered about that.

A place this size needed a housekeeper or a cleaning lady at the least. There was a notice board on the wall beside the fridge. Something you'd see in almost any home. It was empty. Mostly. She stood in front of it and read off the one number handwritten with the name Bettina. "This could be her," she muttered. She pulled out her phone and wrote down the number. She turned to head back to the office and the men when she realized she couldn't see Masters. She peered around the corners. "Masters? Where did you go?"

But he was no longer in the kitchen. Groaning, she walked back toward the men, her phone in her hand, to show them the number. If nothing else, this Bettina might know something of value. She didn't think Michaels would have done his own cleaning. Perhaps he had a cleaning lady?

She could hear the men talking up ahead. She stopped in the middle of the hallway. "Masters? Where are you?"

What was it about cats that they never came when called? She looked around but there was no sign of him again. Then she heard a meow. Loud and close but muffled.

"Masters?"

"Marielle?" Dane stood at the doorway. "What's wrong?"

"Masters," she said. "I just fed him, he disappeared and now I can hear him as if locked in somewhere."

On cue, the cat meowed again. A long plaintiff sound as if he could hear them speak. "He couldn't be back in that downstairs stairway again, could he?"

"Did you open the door again?" Dane walked toward her, his gaze on the wall and the secret door.

"No, I didn't." She turned to look around her as if Masters would magically appear. "So if he's in there then there's another entrance."

"Time to find out." He reopened the secret staircase door.

And Masters hopped out.

"There's your answer." Mason walked toward them. "Obviously we missed something."

"Let's find it," Dane said. He led the way back downstairs.

Marielle grinned. "This is fun."

Mason snorted. "Except we don't know what we're missing and time is short."

She nodded as she raced down the stairs. "I'm thinking there might have been another access point through the lab. It was the only place that was really lived in or the office."

"But why two exits?" Mason asked.

"In case of an accident, I'd think. Chemicals are deadly. In the event of an accident such exits are needed. Even then, in many cases, you're dead."

On that note, they finished the rest of the trip in silence with Dane opening the lab door and walking in. She followed, Mason right behind them. Dane walked to the far end and searched. There was no apparent opening. Not a visible door anywhere.

She stepped back out into the hallway for another look and heard the door slam behind her. She spun to look and the blow came out of the left side. And smashed into her temple. She fell to her knees, her hands sliding down the wall before she collapsed to the floor.

Her gaze was wide in shock at the figure leaning over her.

Dr. Michaels.

DANE WATCHED MARIELLE walk out of the lab. She was enjoying this. Then again most people loved the idea of secret rooms and hidden staircases. The whole treasure hunter mentality. They frustrated him. He wanted to see clearly, and the idea of a house riddled with places like this was irritating as hell.

Still, it put smile on her face so that was good.

The door closed in front of him. Hard.

He frowned and jumped forward the last steps. Had she meant to close it? He reached for the handle but it didn't turn. He threw his weight against it but it wouldn't budge.

"Shit."

"Are we locked in?" Mason asked incredulously. "Really?"

"Apparently." Dane stopped to study the door and had his small tool kit out of his back pocket instantly. "And that means we aren't alone."

"I'm warning the others. Swede can come and get us out."

"No!" Dane said sharply. "Send him after Marielle. Whoever locked us in is likely after her. As she hasn't tried to open the door from the other side, he either has her or she's incapable of opening it. Neither is a great option." He studied the hinges and the lock. As they were in such a secure place, not much attention had been given to the security of the door locks. Perfect.

"I'll have this open in a second." And he went to work on taking the door knob off. When he popped the deadbolt, the door shifted, releasing its tight connections to the door.

"Got it." Mason pulled the door toward them. He peered out and whispered, "She's gone."

Shit.

The two did a quick search of the other rooms. Someone raced down the stairs toward them. They melted into the background. Swede tore around the corner and came to a sliding stop.

"She's gone," Dane said hoarsely. "We have to find her before they go off the grid."

"Shadow has locked down the entrances we know about. And Hawk is outside."

"It's the ones we don't know about that are the problem,"

Mason said. "Masters knows of another way in and out of here, and that's the one we need to find."

"Where is the cat now?" Dane asked, looking around. And there he was on the bottom step of the same stairs that Swede had come down. If he could close off that exit then maybe the cat would lead them to the other one.

He slipped alongside the cat and stepped behind him. Mason walked to the end of the hall. "Masters, come here boy."

Masters sauntered closer. Then lay down, completely disinterested.

"We don't have time for this," Swede said, running his hands along the stone wall. "Why the hell would there be two exits down here anyway."

"There might not be. He could have secreted her out the same way you came down. This house is huge."

"Then let's be methodical and clear it completely."

Moving in unison, they quickly searched the house. Nothing. There were no signs of anyone inside.

Dane's phone buzzed. "Hawk says no one has left the house and there is no movement in the circle of houses. So she's still here."

They spread out and searched the basement again, for the direction she'd been taken. With fear riding him and knowing they were running against the clock, Dane studied the prison cell. There was no point in having two doors to this room. He moved on to the next room and an anomaly caught his eye. The stones at the end of the wall looked to be a different type of rock. He stood in front and studied it. They'd checked it earlier, but as he stared at it now, there was a small, too even, space between the floor and the rock. A mere shadow but there should not be one at all if the rocks were part of the whole system. He ran his fingers over the different formations and his fingers clicked on a metal object. The wall pushed open in front of him.

As if sensing he'd found something, the other two raced toward him. Silently, gun out and down, Dane climbed the new set of stairs.

She was here. He knew it. And he was going to find her.

CHAPTER 28

"THIS WON'T WORK, you know," Marielle said in a conversational tone. "They aren't going to stay locked in."

"Then I'll have to toss in a nice chemical cocktail at them, won't I?" he growled. "This is your fault. No one would have gotten hurt if you'd listened to reason."

"Reason? What are you talking about? You never even talked to me. You pulled a gun on me. And how did you get them to think you were dead?"

"My brother." At her horrified look he added, "I had no choice. The company made it very clear that the same fate awaited me if I didn't come up with a solution to this damn problem. I was desperate."

"You killed your own brother?" She couldn't imagine. Did he not care? Had he no conscience?

"It was his fault. He'd been pissing me off. Came over that day ripping into me for ignoring our mother. Like I had time to worry about the little shit right now. We also looked alike. It used to bug me. Now I found a good use for the similarity."

She shook her head, not quite ready to think that the professor she'd enjoyed conversing with so much was such a psychotic. Thinking he was dead had been easier. She hadn't had time to grieve, but she'd made the mental shift already. Now...all she could do was hope he would die so she'd get out of this mess. Dane would take care of him in a heartbeat – as would any of the other men, but they had to find her first.

He wrenched her to her feet and dragged her down the hall.

"Where are we going?" she asked.

"Out of the house and out of the country. You were such a sentimental fool to come back. And of course you had to pick up Masters and look after him, didn't you?"

"I thought you were dead," she said, outraged. She shoved her hand deep into her pocket, her fingers closing over the tissue she had in there. "I wasn't going to leave him alone, locked up in the house to die."

"Of course not." He shook his head as if she were too stupid to believe. She'd rather he figured that than notice she was shredding the tissue in her pocket and letting the pieces drop out slowly as he dragged her behind him.

"Where are you taking me?"

"The company wants to see you."

Her heart chilled. "What company," she asked hoarsely.

"The name doesn't matter so I'll tell you. It's Hyack, with offices in Germany, and the factory in China They have labs all over the world. They open and then close them down after a few years so tracking is minimized. They have intel from companies all over the world. So much easier for them to stay on top of new discoveries."

"And do they kidnap all chemists," she snapped, realizing this must be the same company Dane and the rest of the SEALs were after.

"Nope, just the ones that have something they want who won't cooperate. You should do your research, my dear. You're in a very dangerous field."

She had no idea. "They can't keep tabs on everyone," she exclaimed. "There are thousands around the world."

"Of course not, but as soon as they get wind of something interesting then they jump on it."

"And what's going to happen to me," she asked, trying to keep him talking so he wouldn't notice the confetti on the floor.

"That's up to you. Cooperate fully or end up like my brother." He sighed. "I really didn't want to have to kill him. Because now I have to deal with my mother alone."

She shook her head wordlessly. Who knew he was so devoid of personal feelings. That there was so little compassion and caring in his heart. He'd always been arrogant and egotistical but then he'd had a lot of accolades all his life and sometimes that got to a person. In this case, apparently he hadn't gotten over himself. And yet while teaching, his passionate love of the subject, his willingness to discuss any aspect of chemistry had endeared him to those of similar passion.

Now she had to wonder if anyone else had the same perspective on him or had the others seen him in a clearer light.

Which would seriously suck and make her judge her own ability to discern character.

"Where are we?" She looked around as it suddenly struck her how unlikely her position was. They were still in the house – or a house. As she hadn't lost consciousness, she knew this wasn't a new location but if this was part of the same house…nothing made sense.

Then she got it. "Is this an underground tunnel?" she asked excitedly. "That's awesome."

"It is a tunnel and it is awesome. I've used it for years. A great way to come and go and not let the lookouts above know what I'm doing."

"How long is it? Does it let out to a road or another house?" She knew she was supposed to be terrified but really...she wasn't. Dane was coming after her. He'd have noticed by now that she was gone. It didn't matter if Michaels had locked them in. That wouldn't stop her SEAL. And he was hers. At least for the moment. And maybe now they could get to the bottom of this nightmare. Besides, this tunnel was wonderful. She reached out a hand to touch the stone wall and marveled at the texture. "It's a magnificent job. I can't imagine how old this is."

"I'm not sure how old it is. It was used to move Jews out of the hands of the Germans, but it existed long before that," he said, keeping a close eye on her. She didn't mind. He'd missed the paper trail she'd left and really he was waving the gun around with a loose grip. He'd killed his brother and was fully prepared to shoot her, but she didn't get the feeling he was planning to kill her. Unless she caused trouble. But she wasn't going to.

At least not yet.

THERE WERE ONLY three steps then a long hallway opened up in front of Dane, round and cold, with a moistness in the air that bespoke of deep underground. He stopped and assessed the danger moving ahead. This wasn't a hall but a tunnel. From the chipped marks on the rocks, it had been hand built. He raced into the darkness, his boots making a strong clipping sound creating an echo as he moved. Immediately he shifted to stealth mode and moved silently. And the echo stopped.

They couldn't be more than twenty minutes ahead of him.

He caught sight of something tiny and white on the stone floor. Then another piece and another. Marielle was leaving a trail for him to follow.

He watched the tiny trail of paper as he raced past. There was a larger one up ahead. He scooped it up as he moved but he never slowed his pace. He turned once to see Swede and Mason behind him. The paper was tissue. He sniffed. Marielle had one in her hands earlier. He smiled. Smart lady.

He picked up the pace and before he took another twenty steps he came up against a blank wall. And knew it was another door. But now that he'd seen the craftsmanship and style, it only took him until Swede and Mason caught up to him to find the mechanism and open the door.

To another tunnel?

He frowned but moved into the newly opened space and realized that this was no longer the same tunnel but now they were in another house. As in the two houses were joined by an underground tunnel. Fascinating, but scary as hell. How far had this asshole taken Marielle? Surely they hadn't had time to get too far.

But now they were in a different house and that meant the likelihood of more people. Were the owners aware of the tunnel? Were they accomplices? Did Michaels own this house as well?

He came to a single wooden door with a silver handle. The door was slightly ajar. He pulled it open slowly and peered around the other side. A big empty room. But tiny pieces of paper sprinkled the steps that wove upward against the left wall.

Marielle.

His heart racing, he ran up the stairs to another room. And voices.

"I don't care what you want me to do," Marielle said, her voice exasperated. "I'm not interested."

"It doesn't matter what you want. My employer wants you, damn it. Now turn around so I can tie your hands behind you."

Dane snuck up on the voices. Relief that she was still okay coursed through him, yet at the same time he wasn't sure why she was being difficult. Then it was Marielle. She was a free spirit.

The man's voice turned ugly. "Now, or I'll knock you out."

Instead of having the effect he wanted, Marielle laughed. "Then I'll be useless. I've had so many head injuries I won't likely survive another one."

"And you won't have to," Dane snapped. "Don't move, asshole. Keep your hands where I can see them." He quickly added, "Marielle get over here."

She tried to get out the way, but the gunman jumped her and held the gun to her head. Then laughed at Dane. "And now what?" He gave Dane a baleful look, shaking Marielle hard. "She's leaving with me."

"No, I'm not," Marielle cried. "I won't. You'll have to shoot me."

"Shut the fuck up," the gunman cried. "I need you to go. The company wants you and what the company wants the company gets."

"I'm not leaving here," she said calmly, staring at Dane. "I will not be a prisoner for the rest of my life."

"We're all prisoners," he cried. "To our bills, our bosses, our taxes, our families. You can't run away."

"No and neither can you," Dane said. "Dr. Michaels, I presume?"

Michaels stared at him in shock…then started to rant his displeasure. "How could she have told you? She didn't have time?"

"She didn't tell me, I figured it out," Dane said, keeping an eye on the man who appeared to be losing the veneer holding him together. "I presume that's a close relative in the morgue."

"His brother," Marielle said. She tried to pull free. The gunman pressed the gun into her temple.

Dane lined the gun up… "Let her go."

"No. I need her. I'm dead without her."

Dane understood but that was too damn bad. "You can't have her."

"Why the fuck not?" Michaels looked close to tears. "Why do you want her?"

Dane didn't answer. "Put the gun down."

Silence.

"I'm asking you to let me have her," Michaels said calmly. Too calmly. "If you won't, then neither of us will get her."

"No," Dane yelled. The look on Michaels' face was that of a man who'd hit the end of his rope. He had to make a fast decision. He lowered his weapon.

CHAPTER 29

"W HY DID YOU do that," Marielle cried as Dane placed the gun on the floor. "Please don't."

"Shut the fuck up, Marielle. I see you've finally met your match, haven't you?" Michaels laughed. "Who'd have thought there would be someone in the world who'd sacrifice himself for you."

And that was exactly what he'd done. Marielle stared wordlessly at Dane, seeing the love in his eyes. The confidence. The knowledge.

She'd trusted him all this time, how could she let him down now?

"I know he would. He loves me," she said quietly. "And I love him. And you will never live to see another day if you try to kidnap me."

Michaels laughed. "I've already got the upper hand here. And isn't that so cute. Love is a lie. A stupid vision that society has gotten sucked into. But it's nothing."

She patted his hand, her smile brightening as she gazed deep into Dane's eyes. "Maybe and maybe you are missing a major piece of DNA that everyone else has. You can't feel joy or love, the same as you can't feel regret or remorse." She lowered her voice. "That's all right, I forgive you."

"What?" Michaels shook his head and tried to drag her backwards, his gaze shocked as he stared at her. "You're fucking nuts."

"Am I?" She watched Dane crouch down on the floor, a message in his eyes as he lifted his jeans' leg.

And she remembered. She gave a slight nod, and with three fingers held out she counted down to two, then one. Then she sat down – hard.

"Wha–" Michaels was blown backwards as the bullet hit him high in the shoulder.

The gun dropped harmlessly. Marielle dove for it, snatched it up, rolled over and pointed it at Michaels. Dane approached, holding his gun back up. Michaels swore profusely. "God damn it, Marielle, what did you do? I'm a dead man now. I'm dead, do you hear me?"

"Having been through the loss once, I'm sure I can stand it," she said, snarling. "After what you've put me through already and the future you were happy to convict me too?" She snorted. "I'm good with that."

"No, you don't understand. They will kill me now." He wavered on his feet, the shock and loss of blood making him weak. Staring at her, he fell to his knees. "I didn't mean for you to get hurt? If you'd willingly been a part of this company, you'd have been fine."

Blood burbled out of his mouth and she realized he was more injured than she'd initially thought. She handed the gun to Dane and ran over to Michaels' side "Easy. We'll get you some help."

He looked at her. "Why?"

"Because you're hurt," she cried out. "I was mad at you for

what you did to me, but I don't want you to die."

"It doesn't matter. But you'll need to get out of here fast. They are coming to pick you up. If I'm alive they'll kill me. If I'm dead, they'll assume you got away."

"Will they come after her again, if that happens?" Dane asked in a harsh tone.

Michaels tried to answer. "Library. Bottom shelf. Journals of the company. Use them. Bring it down." He collapsed to the ground, her hand bracing him as the blood pumped sluggishly at a steady rate. Something vital had been nicked. She watched the blood, wishing the medics would arrive faster. She held her hand over the wound but the blood slowly pumped between her fingers. "They take out all resistance before it can grow. Anyone and everything." He gasped slowly.

"Did they have a lab in Italy?" Dane asked, remembering the innocent man gunned down on the road after talking to Mason.

Michaels nodded, whispered, "Not anymore." He coughed once then again. "They buy, use the place for a few years then ditch it. They've already silenced everyone that had anything to do with the deal. They take out any one they believe is working against them." This time when he coughed, he couldn't stop and his weak body shook in pain.

"Easy," Marielle said, "Help is coming."

"Not in time," Michaels groaned.

"I'll find the journals. We'll bring them down," she promised.

"Good." Michaels' gaze shifted to Dane. "Is she right?"

Dane frowned but crouched beside the dying man. "Right about what?"

"Do you love her?"

Marielle watched the start of surprise jolt through Dane. But he answered quickly, "Yes, I love her."

Really? Oh Lord. It was a hell of a time for this subject matter.

"Good. Then protect her. She's onto a brilliant idea. This won't be the last time someone comes after her."

Dane leaned closer. "How do we keep her safe?"

Michaels now leaned against Marielle, his breath harsh, strained, whispered, "It's all in the journals. Find them. Use them. Keep her safe." He took a long rattling breath…and died.

In Marielle's arms.

Many hours later they stood outside the military airport in the cool air. They were going stateside. Finally. It had been a very long, hard day. There was a mess to clean up, but the Germans would take care of it. The journals were being taken to the joint task force that would work together to bring down the ones behind the scenes.

Marielle stood outside the plane and stared up at the sky. Dane wasn't here yet. He'd been in the last vehicle. She hoped the plane would wait for him but knew it wasn't a guarantee.

"Marielle, come inside."

She nodded and let Mason lead her to a seat at the front. Moments later she was buckled in with the engines warming up.

So this was how it was going to end. No Dane. No Masters. No one had seen the cat since Michaels had taken her captive. Nothing to show for her week long holiday but the memories – both good and bad.

Tired and immeasurably sad, she leaned her head back and closed her eyes. She refused to cry. The damn tears could wait until she got home. That was when she'd let it all pour out. Not until then. But saying so didn't make it so. She sniffled and wiped her eyes. Damn it. That big lug had better look her up when they made it home.

Without warning, the plane door opened suddenly and Dane raced in.

She stared at him in shocked surprise then delight as he placed one very familiar cat carrier on her lap. One very large tomcat stared at her and said, "Meow."

"Masters!" she wrapped her arms around the carrier and hugged it. She laughed, but tears of happiness leaked through. "I thought I'd lost you this time."

"We finally got clearance based on the reading of the will the first time," Dane said from beside her. "But I had a devil of a time catching him. He didn't like all the strangers in the house."

"That's all right. I didn't either." She reached over and grasped his arm. "Thank you," she said warmly. "I'm so happy you found him."

He nodded, stared at her and opened his mouth as if to say something then snapped his jaw closed.

"What?" she asked curiously.

"Did you mean it?"

She frowned. "Mean what?"

"What you said back there?"

"Ah that." She grinned and realized what the hell, after all they'd been through, she might as well be honest. Besides, it was the only way she knew to be. "Absolutely."

A light grew deep in his eyes. He leaned closer. His breath was warm on her cheek, the tender look in his eyes melting her heart. "We haven't known each other for long."

"Long enough for me to know all I need to know about

you," she whispered. "Unless you need more time."

"Oh I do. I need all the time in the world – with you."

And he kissed her. In the back of the plane someone yelled, "Finally."

"About time."

"Yay."

"Go, Dane."

She chuckled. She was fine with that. They were her family now too. And families did things like this.

As long as she had Dane. It was all good.

"Does that mean we can go home now?" she whispered after he lifted his head.

"Oh yeah. Home, a hot shower, good food and a big bed just for the two of us."

She grinned. "Sounds perfect." The plane finished taxiing at that moment and lifted into the air. "I can't wait."

The future was ahead of them. And it was damn near perfect.

This concludes Book 3 of SEALs of Honor: Dane.

Book 4 is available.

Swede: SEALs of Honor, Book 4

Buy this book at your favorite vendor.

SEALs of Honor Series

Mason: SEALs of Honor, Book 1

Hawk: SEALs of Honor, Book 2

Dane: SEALs of Honor, Book 3

Swede: SEALs of Honor, Book 4

Shadow: SEALs of Honor, Book 5

Cooper: SEALs of Honor, Book 6

Author's Note

Thank you for reading Dane: SEALs of Honor, Book 3! If you enjoyed the book, please take a moment and leave a short review.

Dear reader,

I love to hear from readers, and you can contact me at my website: www.dalemayer.com or at my Facebook author page. To be informed of new releases and special offers, sign up for my newsletter. And if you are interested in joining my street team, here is the Facebook sign up page.

Cheers,
Dale Mayer

Touched by Death

Adult RS/thriller

Get this book at your favorite vendor.

Death had touched anthropologist Jade Hansen in Haiti once before, costing her an unborn child and perhaps her very sanity.

A year later, determined to face her own issues, she returns to Haiti with a mortuary team to recover the bodies of an American family from a mass grave. Visiting his brother after the quake, independent contractor Dane Carter puts his life on hold to help the sleepy town of Jacmel rebuild. But he finds it hard to like his brother's pregnant wife or her family. He wants to go home, until he meets Jade – and realizes what's missing in his own life. When the mortuary team begins work, it's as if malevolence has been released from the earth. Instead of laying her ghosts to rest, Jade finds herself confronting death and terror again.

And the man who unexpectedly awakens her heart – is right in the middle of it all.

By Death Series

Vampire in Denial

This is book 1 of the Family Blood Ties Saga

Get this book at your favorite vendor.

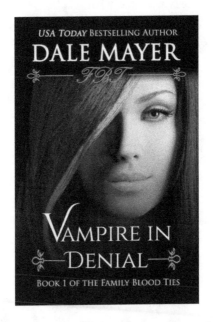

Blood doesn't just make her who she is...it also makes her what she is.

Like being a sixteen-year-old vampire isn't hard enough, Tessa's throwback human genes make her an outcast among her relatives. But try as she might, she can't get a handle on the vampire lifestyle and all the...blood.

Turning her back on the vamp world, she embraces the human teenage lifestyle—high school, peer pressure and finding a boyfriend. Jared manages to stir something in her blood. He's smart and fun and oh, so cute. But Tessa's dream of a having the perfect boyfriend turns into a nightmare when vampires attack the movie theatre and kidnap her date.

Once again, Tessa finds herself torn between the human world and the vampire one. Will blood own out? Can she make peace with who she is as well as what?

Warning: This book ends with a cliffhanger! Book 2 picks up where this book ends.

Family Blood Ties Series

Vampire in Denial – FREE

Vampire in Distress

Vampire in Design

Vampire in Deceit

Vampire in Defiance

Vampire in Conflict

Vampire in Chaos

Vampire in Crisis

Vampire in Control

Family Blood Ties 3in1

Sian's Solution – A Family Blood Ties Short Story

Broken Protocols

Get this book at your favorite vendor.

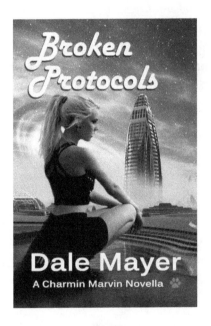

Dani's been through a year of hell...

Just as it's getting better, she's tossed forward through time with her orange Persian cat, Charmin Marvin, clutched in her arms. They're dropped into a few centuries into the future. There's nothing she can do to stop it, and it's impossible to go back.

And then it gets worse...

A year of government regulation is easing, and Levi Blackburn is feeling back in control. If he can keep his reckless brother in check, everything will be perfect. But while he's been protecting Milo from the government, Milo's been busy working on a present for him...

The present is Dani, only she comes with a snarky cat who suddenly starts talking...and doesn't know when to shut up.

In an age where breaking protocols have severe consequences, things go wrong, putting them all in danger...

Charmin Marvin Romantic Comedy Series

About the Author

Dale Mayer is a USA Today bestselling author best known for her Psychic Visions and Family Blood Ties series. Her contemporary romances are raw and full of passion and emotion (Second Chances, SKIN), her thrillers will keep you guessing (By Death series), and her romantic comedies will keep you giggling (It's a Dog's Life and Charmin Marvin Romantic Comedy series).

She honors the stories that come to her – and some of them are crazy and break all the rules and cross multiple genres!

To go with her fiction, she also writes nonfiction in many different fields with books available on resume writing, companion gardening and the US mortgage system. She has recently published her Career Essentials Series. All her books are available in print and ebook format.

Connect with Dale Mayer Online

Dale's Website – www.dalemayer.com
Twitter – @DaleMayer
Facebook – facebook.com/DaleMayer.author

Also by Dale Mayer

Published Adult Books:

Psychic Vision Series

Tuesday's Child – FREE

Hide'n Go Seek

Maddy's Floor

Garden of Sorrow

Knock, Knock...

Rare Find

Eyes to the Soul

Now You See Her

Psychic Visions 3in1

By Death Series

Touched by Death – Part 1 – FREE

Touched by Death – Part 2

Touched by Death – Parts 1&2

Haunted by Death

Chilled by Death

Second Chances...at Love Series

Second Chances – Part 1 – FREE

Second Chances – Part 2

Second Chances – complete book (Parts 1 & 2)

Charmin Marvin Romantic Comedy Series

Broken Protocols

Broken Protocols 2

Broken Protocols 3

Broken Protocols 3.5

Broken Protocols 1-3

Broken and... Mending

Skin

Scars

Scales (of Justice)

Glory

Genesis

Tori

Celeste

Biker Blues

Biker Blues: Morgan, Part 1

Biker Blues: Morgan, Part 2

Biker Blues: Morgan, Part 3

SEALs of Honor

Mason: SEALs of Honor, Book 1

Hawk: SEALs of Honor, Book 2

Dane: SEALs of Honor, Book 3

Swede: SEALs of Honor, Book 4

Shadow: SEALs of Honor, Book 5

Cooper: SEALs of Honor, Book 6

Collections

Dare to Be You…

Dare to Love…

Dare to be Strong…

RomanceX3

Standalone Novellas

It's a Dog's Life

Riana's Revenge

Published Young Adult Books:

Family Blood Ties Series

Vampire in Denial – FREE

Vampire in Distress

Vampire in Design

Vampire in Deceit

Vampire in Defiance

Vampire in Conflict

Vampire in Chaos

Vampire in Crisis

Vampire in Control

Family Blood Ties 3in1

Sian's Solution – A Family Blood Ties Short Story

Design series
Dangerous Designs – FREE
Deadly Designs
Darkest Designs
Design Series Trilogy

Standalone
In Cassie's Corner
Gem Stone (a Gemma Stone Mystery)
Time Thieves

Published Non-Fiction Books:

Career Essentials
Career Essentials: The Résumé
Career Essentials: The Cover Letter
Career Essentials: The Interview
Career Essentials: 3 in 1